A DOG'S PORPOISE

A DOG'S PORPOISE

M. C. ROSS

Scholastic Inc.

All rights reserved. Published by Scholastic Inc., *Publishers since 1920.* SCHOLASTIC and associated logos are trademarks and/or registered trademarks of Scholastic Inc.

The publisher does not have any control over and does not assume any responsibility for author or third-party websites or their content.

ISBN 978-1-338-26397-8

10 9 8 7 6 5 4 3 2 1   19 20 21 22 23

Printed in the U.S.A.   40
First printing January 2019

Book design by Nina Goffi

Dedicated to Liffey, and also to Spree.

CHAPTER ONE

Bangor

Puff!

Bangor's favorite sound had always been one he made himself: the sound of his own breathing. Because Bangor was a harbor porpoise, he didn't have to breathe too often—in fact, one time he had stayed underwater for ten whole minutes, just to prove to his older brother, Belfast, that he could.

But he *preferred* to come up for air as often as possible. He enjoyed the brief break of the above-water world, his blowhole spurting away all the slick salt water on the surface of his back—*puff!*—before pushing out his old breath and drawing in a new one, all in a split second. Then his dorsal fin arced up and out and back into the ocean, and Bangor was on his way back down until he decided he wanted to resurface again. Breathing kept him alive, of course, but more importantly, it was fun. And that was life all over for a harbor porpoise; being alive was more or less the exact same thing as having fun.

And now that he was thinking about breathing, he decided to do it again.

Puff!

But this time, as Bangor plunged back down, he got a surprise. At three hundred feet below the surface, a gray flash rocketed past his right flank, so close that bubbles exploded across Bangor's field of vision. He spun to the left and released a rapid burst of sonar clicks to signal his confusion. The sound waves raced through the roiling water, bounced off the source of whatever had shocked him, and returned to Bangor's ears in a matter of milliseconds. The moment Bangor heard what was in front of him, all of his confusion disappeared.

There, rolling in front of him playfully, was Belfast. Belfast loved teasing his little brother, and since Bangor was the oddball of the family, Belfast had always found plenty to tease him about. Whether it was Bangor going to the surface too often, or swimming off without a moment's notice because he was lost in another daydream, Belfast was always there to keep him in check.

Well, two can play at that game, thought Bangor. He darted forward as fast as he could, and he was satisfied to see Belfast's left eye widen in shock just before Bangor caught up with him, swimming in tight circles over and under his older brother, releasing a cyclone of bubbles. Then Belfast joined in the dance, and all ill will was forgotten as the two of them shot off across the water, playing and clicking giddily, looping around each other at breakneck speed.

Some days, Bangor didn't feel like the family oddball. Some days, he felt like his entire family was just as odd as he was, and he loved it.

"Eee-eee-ee-ee-e-e-e?"

And there were the rest of the oddballs, right on cue. Bangor and Belfast slowed their pace at the sound of the traditional harbor porpoise greeting, and Bangor shot off the proper series of clicks to say hello back: He started off low and slow, and then increased the frequency higher and higher in a chipper upsweep:

"*Eee-eee-ee-ee-e-e-e!*"

This got a delighted spin from their youngest sister, Bristol, and a lazy flap of the tail from their uncle York. Uncle York wasn't much for frolicking or playing, but he was *very* much for eating frequently and in large quantities.

And there, bringing up the rear as always, was Bangor's mother, Kittery. She didn't hang back because she was the slowest swimmer of the pod—that was absolutely York, who had once eaten so many mackerel that Bangor had to push him along with his snout for a few miles while York regained his senses. If Kittery had wanted to, she could have swum circles around York, but instead she chose to keep her pod safe by making sure they were all within sight whenever possible. And now here they all were, united under her watchful—but clearly amused—gaze.

"*Ee-ee-ee!*" Kittery chirped.

Now that all of them were there, Bangor clicked again—not because he had anything to say, but just because he was happy. He knew that not every porpoise had a pod like this. In fact, most of the harbor porpoises he'd met in his two years of life had been loners, just passing through this little northern patch of the Atlantic that Bangor thought of as home. But Kittery had always made a point of keeping her kids together, and York was far too lazy to live on his own, so a family pod had formed, and Bangor didn't think he'd trade that family for anything.

Well. Maybe for *one* thing.

Bangor had always been, by far, the most adventurous member of his family, ready to swim off or up or in any direction that seemed like it might contain fun or new friends or even new fish to eat. Everyone in the pod loved him dearly, but they all had their own reasons for staying put. Belfast scorned anything that was different from the norm; baby Bristol just couldn't keep up; Kittery was far too cautious to endorse that sort of adventuring; and even Uncle York couldn't be persuaded to swim out to new feeding grounds, clearly reasoning that a fish in the beak was worth two in the deep, and half the hassle, to boot.

Just once, Bangor would have liked to go on a real trip somewhere to find something new, or to make a new friend. But harbor porpoises tended to find one place to live and stay there, and while there was plenty that was odd about Bangor's pod, in this respect, they were happy to conform to the norm.

And no matter what, Bangor was happy to be with his pod.

"E-e-e-e-e."

Kittery's rapid-fire clicking interrupted Bangor's reverie. Bangor was very familiar with that clicking, especially from his mother. It was the sound of a warning—a heads-up that something was wrong—and Kittery's calm but insistent loops around the perimeter of the pod were a clear signal that she wanted them to pay attention to their surroundings. But what was Bangor supposed to be looking for? He echolocated as far into the distance as he could, and was surprised to hear something large and unfamiliar coming toward them from far away; but he was even more surprised to see Kittery shaking her head. He knew what that meant: *That's not what I'm worried about.*

Bangor focused harder, listening for any other new threats in the nearby water. Then he realized—it was the *water* itself! The water pressure all around them had dropped. Bangor had been so caught up in playing and dreaming—and the change had been so gradual at first—that he hadn't noticed it was happening. But now it was falling quickly enough that everyone could feel it. That, and the dark surface of the water, churning cloudy black where there should have been moonlight, could mean only one thing:

A storm was coming. And it was big.

Bangor's pride at figuring out the puzzle quickly gave way to nervousness over the danger this storm might bring. Even deep underwater, big storms could cause chaos. They often brought roiling waves violent enough to batter smaller fish in all kinds of directions; they changed the ocean's salt and oxygen levels in ways that were unpredictable and dangerous; and if the storm was strong enough, it could dredge things up from the bottom of the ocean, flinging seafloor sediment or even shipwrecks into the paths of unsuspecting animals.

The luckiest sea creatures were the ones who were smart enough to know what was coming and fast enough to get away before things got really bad. Harbor porpoises were definitely fast, and they were *definitely* smart. So now, Bangor realized giddily, they would go somewhere else—somewhere *new*. Bangor was about to get his wish!

Chittering excitedly, Bangor shot a few hundred feet south, and then rapidly returned to look at his pod expectantly: *This way! Let's go this way!* They'd never really ventured south before; harbor porpoises tended to stay where it was cold year-round, and this seemed like the perfect time to give it a try.

But Bangor's mother shook her head again, patiently indicating the other direction: *We always go north; we'll go north now.*

Bangor huffed, releasing a stream of bubbles that floated up to the surface, which was beginning to dapple with rainwater. The edge of the storm was arriving, and they didn't have much time for debate. Still, Bangor didn't know when he'd get another chance at a trip like this, and he was determined to make it count.

He flipped around again, emitting a high-pitched squeak: *Pleeease? It could be fun!* Bristol, ever the impressionable little sister, got in on the act, flipping and wheedling like her life depended on it. Kittery turned to Uncle York, looking for some support, but he just gave his customary neutral flap. For a lazy porpoise like Uncle York, all movement was equally unpleasant, no matter what direction it was in.

Bangor clicked eagerly at Belfast, hoping his older brother could provide a deciding vote. But something had caused Belfast to become distracted. His attention was focused on something farther off from the pod, to the north. Bangor bumped up against his flank: *Hey. Buddy. Over here.* But Belfast brushed him away, moving a few feet farther out from the pod, echolocating ever more intently off into the distance.

The waves above them were getting bigger now, and Bangor was starting to get nervous. He wondered if he should let the whole thing go, and he also wondered what could possibly have his brother so concerned. Then he clicked in the direction his brother was clicking, and stopped wondering.

A gigantic wall of high-pitched sound was coming toward them—the sound Bangor had detected earlier, but closer now, and pitched at a volume that could only mean one thing: boats. Human boats, and big ones. The kind that made sound waves that knocked porpoises way out of whack. For a harbor porpoise navigating by echolocation, swimming close to one of these ships was just like having a blinding light shone into your eyes, and just as likely to make a porpoise lose track of where they were, or even run into something—hard. And from the cacophony coming their way, this wasn't just one ship, it was a whole fleet of them. They didn't normally come this close to the pod's part of the ocean, but the storm must have been driving them back to land, forcing them to take an unexpected route. If Bangor and his family tried to swim past that fleet, there was no guarantee they'd get where they wanted to go as one pod, let alone in one piece.

As the ships drew ever closer, Kittery appeared to make a judgment call. She darted south—the direction that would take them away from the ships, and the same way Bangor had wanted to go. It was a victory for Bangor, but by now he was almost too nervous to enjoy it. As he began to follow his mother, he hoped they could swim fast enough to escape disaster.

But just as they were making headway, a large wave rolled over them, pulling Bristol backward. She squeaked loudly in fright, and Belfast and Kittery instantly lunged after her. Even Uncle York made a motion to go after the youngest member of the pod. But as Bangor watched in horror, Uncle York began what should have been a straight shot toward Bristol, and then unexpectedly veered hard to the side. There had been nothing in front of him, but he'd still reared up and away, as if frightened of something only he could see or hear.

It was the ships, Bangor realized. They were already upon the pod.

And so was the storm.

Another strong wave tore through the water, and this time it was strong enough that not just Bristol was affected. Bangor, Belfast, and Kittery were all rolled several yards to the side. Only Uncle York, the heaviest of the group, was strong enough to stay mostly in place, and even then, he was so disoriented by the ships that he was essentially swimming in circles. Things were going downstream, and fast. Bangor tried to rely on his eyesight rather than his echolocation, but silt was beginning to kick up from the ocean floor, and it was getting harder and harder to see. Then, as the first ship rolled overhead, it became impossible. The ship, taller and larger than Bangor had imagined, blocked out any light from above the surface of the water, and everything around Bangor went dark.

With his senses stripped away, Bangor was left with pure instinct. All he could do was go to the last place he'd seen his family going, so he pointed himself south—at least, he hoped it was south—and swam as fast and as hard as he could. As he propelled himself through the turbulent waters, he clicked as loudly as possible, hoping against hope that a member of his family might hear him.

But if anyone did, he didn't hear them respond, and he couldn't stop to wait for them to do so. He had to outswim these boats, and then he had to outswim the storm—and it wasn't going to be easy.

Bangor swam faster than he thought he knew how and longer than he'd ever swum before. Just minutes ago, he'd been able to breathe for the sheer joy of it. But now he didn't want to come up to the surface until he knew the boats were well behind him, even as he got closer to the ten-minute mark and his lungs began to burn. The water was still choppy, but the roar of the boats was getting dimmer. Or was he just becoming light-headed without fresh air? After what felt like an eternity, Bangor couldn't take it anymore. If he went up to the surface, he might run into a ship, but if he stayed down here, he would *definitely* run out of air. He had to take the risk.

It was the most excited Bangor had ever been about taking a breath, and that was saying something. He altered his course swiftly, still swimming south, but now also racing up through the water, getting closer to the dark and choppy surface of the waves, closer, closer . . .

Puff!

It was the best breath Bangor had ever taken, and he inhaled as much as his lungs would allow. As he dipped back down below the surface, he realized something else that made it even better: The boats were gone! He'd raced them, and he'd won! Bangor immediately went back for another breath, just to celebrate, just because he could. Belfast would be so impressed when he heard about this.

Belfast. His brother. His family.

All celebration ceased as Bangor turned, clicking curiously: *Hello? Anyone?*

But no one was there. Just him and the still-stormy waves, in an unfamiliar part of the ocean that he'd never even seen before. His family had lost him.

No, Bangor thought. *I've lost my family.*

But it wasn't like being *totally* lost, was it? He knew where he was: south. The place he'd always wanted to go. And nobody was here to tell him not to go any farther.

At that thought, Bangor felt a pang of guilt. He didn't know where his pod was, or even if they were safe. Would Bristol be okay in those big waves? Had slow-swimming Uncle York found his way out from under the ships? There was no way for Bangor to know.

But there was one thing he did know: The last direction he'd gotten from his mother was to swim south. That was what the whole pod had been told to do.

If you're going to meet them anywhere, whispered a voice in the back of Bangor's brain, *it's going to be down here. Maybe even farther. You'll all just keep swimming until you find one another.* And in the meantime, if Bangor got to enjoy some new sights and sounds, maybe even some new fish . . . would that be so bad?

It was a question that Bangor didn't actually want to think too hard about. Luckily, he didn't have to just yet. Right now, the only thing he had to do was get farther away from those boats and these choppy waves. With a growing sense of nervous excitement, Bangor turned himself south again, and hoped that his family was doing the same—wherever they were.

As he struck out on his own, he realized there was one other thing he had to do right now—or really just wanted to do:

Puff!

CHAPTER TWO

Natalie

Whumph.

When Natalie Prater was a little girl, she would make waves in the bathtub and shout, "Splash! Splash!"

Now that she was twelve, though, she knew a real wave—an ocean wave, the kind crashing below her now—didn't just make a cute little splash. It made a sound you could *feel*, beating off the side of a boat and shuddering up through your legs and all the way to your teeth. It wasn't a splash. It was a *whumph*. Natalie thought it might be her favorite sound.

"Natalie!" her father yelled from the wheelhouse. "I told you to stay away from the side of the boat while we're moving!"

But from the way he said it, he clearly knew that he was going to have to tell her again, and sooner rather than later. Natalie didn't think there was any point to being on a boat unless you were leaning half out the side, feeling the *whumph* and the *crash* and the sea spray in your face. And while her father might have worried about her, he himself was a lifelong fisherman, and he knew full well how enticing the sea could be, even on a cold, gray day like today.

Still, Natalie moved to the center of the deck, looking down over the puffy folds of her life vest and moving carefully so as not to trip over any fishing nets or tackle boxes. She knew her father was doing her a favor by taking her out on the water today, and there was no use in getting him all worked up about boat safety.

Especially not once he figured out the secret thing that Natalie had done. He'd have plenty to get worked up about then.

"Alright, this should be far enough." Her father cut the engine, allowing the boat to slow down dramatically. The *whumph* of the waves died down and gave way to the gentle slosh of the almost-open ocean. It was a moment Natalie normally loved, but now it made her gulp, because it meant she was that much closer to having her secret discovered.

Together, Natalie and her father had spent many sunny, beautiful days out here on the Prater family fishing boat, the *Maria P*. But today was not one of those days. Not that it wasn't beautiful in its own way—there was always something magical about seeing storm clouds gather out on the open ocean—but it certainly wasn't sunny. Instead, a curtain of rain was sweeping toward them from well beyond the farthest point of Perkins Cove. Perhaps that was why none of the other fishermen of Ogunquit, Maine, were out on the water today, but it was also exactly how Natalie had convinced her father to take her out on the boat.

"You told me water pressure drops before a storm, right?" Natalie had said that morning over breakfast. "And that's when all the fish come out to see what's up."

"That's not *exactly* how it works," her father had responded, pouring milk into his cereal bowl. "But fishing can often be best in the hour right before a storm, yes."

"Then it's a perfect time to go! You could trawl that low-pressure system and catch *so* many fish!" Natalie knew all the best methods for swaying her father, and demonstrating that she'd been paying attention to his lectures about fishing was chief among them. Nevertheless, she'd held her breath, watching carefully as her father stared down at his cereal bowl and considered her words.

"Alright," he'd said finally. "I suppose I could use the extra haul. Maybe then I could be eating name-brand cereal, instead of these Bran Crisps."

She'd leaped up from the table and given her father a big hug.

"But you have to help with the nets!"

So now Natalie was helping with the nets, throwing them over each side of the deck like her father had taught her, while he kept a calm hand on the helm and propelled them slowly but surely across the outer reaches of Perkins Cove. She couldn't see his face, but she could hear him humming, and that made Natalie smile, because if her father was humming, that usually meant *he* was wearing a smile. He really did light up whenever she took an interest in his work. It made him happier about everything. Or, at least, she really hoped it would.

Thump.

The sound came from the side of the boat, but it wasn't the sound of a wave. It had come from inside one of the two long coolers that lined each side of the deck, waiting for fish to fill them up. Except, based on that noise, one of them was already full.

Thump. Skritch.

"What was that?" Mr. Prater asked.

"What was what?" Natalie asked back.

Her cheeks burned bright red. How had he heard that from all the way up at the front of the boat, and over the sound of the motor, to boot? Maybe it was true what they said about fishermen—they really did know everything that happened on their ship.

Oh, well. This had always been inevitable.

Skritch. Skritch. Tha-thump.

"Hrrmph!"

"That!" Mr. Prater turned his head from the helm now, looking back at the deck. "Do you really not hear that?"

"I'm not sure . . ." Natalie faltered midsentence. The lid of the fish cooler to her starboard side was starting to bounce up and down now, which shouldn't have been possible—unless it had been slightly open the whole time.

Mr. Prater's eyes narrowed.

"Natalie," he said. "You didn't."

"Listen—" Natalie began.

And then the lid of the cooler shot open, and out popped an extremely friendly face.

"Oh my gosh!" Natalie cried, as convincingly as she could. "There's a *dog* on the boat!"

"Natalie," her father groaned, then sighed.

"Hrrmph!" the dog snorted, panting with happy excitement at having made his way out of his fishy kennel. *"Rrff!"*

"Hello, Lars," Mr. Prater said wearily.

"He must have snuck into the cooler before we took off!" Natalie said, just like she'd rehearsed it that morning in front of her bathroom mirror. "Maybe he smelled some fish from your last time out, and . . . and he thought he could get a taste, and then the lid fell sort of closed, but not all the way closed, because then he'd be suffocated, and but so then—"

Shhmph. The engine cut completely, and her father turned to face her, his hands on his hips. The boat rocked a little in the sudden stillness, and Mr. Prater had to adopt a comically wide stance to keep from falling over, but the expression on his face was no joke at all.

"You put him in there," he said. "You emptied out the cooler, and you threw in a treat, and you got Lars to jump in there and stow away with us until we were too far out for me to make him swim back. At least, it *better* have been a treat. You *better* have blasted that cooler out with a hose before Lars got in there. Because if he *actually* went in there for the fish smell, and now *actually* smells like fish, then I am *not* letting him come home with us when we get back to shore, which we will be doing *immediately*."

"But, *Dad*—" Natalie started to protest, and regretted it instantly. Any argument that began with "But,

Dad" was practically destined to lose. She could do better than that.

"This can't keep happening," Mr. Prater said. "When you brought Lars home, I told you we could feed him a few times. But we can't just take a stray in off the street, and we *certainly* can't take him out on the open water. Has he ever even been on a boat before?"

"He has *now*," Natalie pointed out, trying to sound reasonable. "That's why I thought he should come with us. I thought maybe if you saw how good he was—"

Mr. Prater rubbed his temples. "I never said Lars wasn't a good dog, Natalie," he said. "I just don't know if we can keep him."

Natalie crossed her arms and sat down on the other fish cooler. Lars took the opportunity to scrabble across the deck toward her and lick the salty seawater off her face.

Why couldn't Dad see how amazing Lars was? It had been apparent to Natalie from the first moment she'd spotted him last week, standing outside the Coveside Café, greeting the people who came out the front door. He had obviously been a very hungry dog, and he didn't have a collar on, and Natalie had heard reports lately about a stray mutt who'd been spotted around Ogunquit. But every time someone left the café who might have fed him something, he got so caught up in greeting them with a wagging tail and a panting smile that he completely forgot to stay focused on the food in their hands. He was too loving for his own good. How could you *not* fall for a dog like that?

And for that matter, how could you not bring Lars back to the shack where you lived with your father and announce that you needed to get this dog some dinner—and fast—and also maybe some breakfast the next morning and dinner again, and then again every day after for the rest of all time?

To Mr. Prater's credit, he had gone down to the freezer and made dinner for the dog out of some haddock he hadn't sold. And Mr. Prater had even let the dog sleep by their front door that night, and fed him leftover fish heads the next morning, even as he insisted they were going to have to kick the stray out any time now.

But the second Natalie knew she had a fighting chance was when her father named him Lars.

"What kind of dog do you think he is?" Natalie had asked that first morning, trying to stall before they had to send Lars back out into the unseasonably chilly April air.

"I don't think he's any one kind of dog," her father had said, surveying the stray animal thoughtfully. He wasn't a small dog by any means, but he'd been made wiry by hunger, and much of his messy brown fur was turning gray at the edges. Lars, who was just finishing his fish heads, chose that moment to look up at Mr. Prater with an expression so expectant it practically spoke: *Well?*

"He doesn't even look like a dog at all," Mr. Prater laughed. "He looks like an old man."

It was true. Lars's eyes were alive with love and curiosity, but those brown-and-gray whiskers tufting out from his snout framed his face in a perfect old man's beard.

"You look like an old fisherman," Mr. Prater said, reaching down to scratch behind the dog's ears. "Like a Lars. Is your name Lars?"

Maybe it was the scratching, or the fish heads, but in that moment, Natalie's new friend smiled wide and spoke: *"Rrff!"* And that's how Lars became Lars.

And Natalie became convinced that her father could be won over.

So she'd waited a week while she hatched her plan, and now here she was on the boat with Lars standing up on her lap, and her father's approval hanging in the balance.

"Please don't make us go in right away," she said. "Look—we're not even moving and the nets are filling up!"

It was true. The ropes that tied the net down to the side of the deck were tugging gently as they loaded up with fish.

"I don't know," Mr. Prater said, looking out over the water. "We don't even know if Lars can swim. And that storm's coming in faster than I thought. Listen, Natalie, even if I wanted to keep Lars around, it'd be harder now than ever. Maybe if your—"

He stopped, but Natalie knew what would have come next: *If your mother was still here.* Natalie's mother would have gladly helped take care of any dogs, but she didn't live with Natalie and her father anymore. She was the Maria P. that the boat was named after, but she dropped the *P* last year when she and Mr. Prater divorced, saying she needed some time to be on her own. Mr. Prater handled it as best as he could, but Natalie knew that sometimes he got overwhelmed—especially in the past few months, when Natalie's mother moved in with Bob Dugnutt, aka Diver Bob, the corny guy who lived right by the ocean and took tourist families out on his boat to crack jokes and show them starfish and lobsters. These days, it was looking more and more like the former Maria P. might become Maria D., as in Dugnutt.

Normally, thinking about this would have made Natalie feel overwhelmed, too. But in this moment, it also presented her with an opening.

"A promise is a promise," Natalie said, sticking out her chin. "You told me that. And *you* promised me we'd go out on the water today. And *I* promised Nancy Jane I'd take pictures of the storm for her paintings.

And the weatherman promised us we had until six before that storm hit the harbor."

The guilt-seeking missile worked like a charm. Natalie could see her father's expression soften. But the concern in his gaze didn't go away.

"Okay," he said. "I'll let the nets out a bit more, and you can take a few pictures. But it really *is* getting choppy out here, so we can't stay *too* long. I want you to remember that a promise is absolutely a promise— except when it's from the weatherman."

Or when it's your mom, promising she'll stay with you forever, Natalie thought darkly. But she knew that that kind of talk wouldn't be helpful right now. And besides, her father was right. The storm was bearing down on them with unexpected speed, and she'd have to act fast if she wanted to get those photos.

As Mr. Prater slowly restarted the engine, Lars woofed happily and leaped around his feet, obviously excited by the new experience of being free to roam on a moving boat. The sight gave Natalie a small swell of joy, and as she fished her phone out of her pocket, she made sure to take a photo of her dad and dog, happy together. Hopefully, soon, life could be like this all the time.

Then a large wave rocked the boat a little, and Natalie had to sit down to steady her grip on the camera. She wanted to get good photos of the storm clouds for Nancy Jane, who lived next door and made paintings of the local scenery to hang in the Coveside Café. If Natalie's reference photos were good enough, sometimes Nancy Jane would buy her a delicious pastry from the café—and now, Natalie thought, maybe if her photos were *really* good, she could score an extra pastry for Lars.

Lars, for his part, was having the time of his life, sniffing all the strange new objects on the boat and dancing back and forth on his paws every time a particularly strong wave rocked the deck, which was happening more and more frequently as the minutes went on. The storm was coming in awfully fast now. Natalie had been so focused on trying to capture the boiling, roiling clouds as perfectly as possible that she hadn't really realized just how close those clouds were getting, until a drop of rain plopped onto the screen of her waterproof phone case. She blinked and used the sleeve of her sweatshirt to wipe the water away, and as she did so, she noticed what she'd been too caught up to notice before. The clouds were filling up the entire frame now. They were *here*.

"Alright," Mr. Prater called from the wheelhouse, clearly noticing the same thing. "That should be a good haul—no need to push it any further." He cut the engine again. "Let's get those nets in, fast."

Natalie nodded, pocketing her phone and bracing herself on the port side of the deck. She had plenty of experience by now at helping her father haul nets in and dump them out, but today felt different. For one, the hauls her father was pulling up were as heavy as she'd ever seen them. And with the boat rocking more and more, it was no easy feat helping him dump the massive quantities of flopping fish into the portside cooler. But there was one other thing that neither of the Praters were used to: Lars, barking inquisitively as net after net of fish poured past. Apparently recognizing the smell of his new favorite breakfast food, Lars even went so far as to hop up on the edge of the cooler and poke his head inside. Natalie hurried to pull Lars away, but that just convinced him that she wanted to play—which, normally, would have been delightful, if things weren't getting so dicey on deck.

"Natalie!" her father yelled over the wind and the waves. "Make sure Lars stays away from the side of the boat!"

Even Natalie had to admit that was a good idea, and as they finished up on the port side of the boat, she tried to keep Lars from following them all the way starboard. But when Lars saw them move toward the starboard cooler, he recognized the same cooler that he'd stowed away in just an hour ago, and happily leaped to dive in.

Except the cooler wasn't open; the lid was shut tight on top.

And it was wet and slick from the rain.

And the *Maria P.* was about to be rocked by its biggest wave yet.

As Natalie watched helplessly, Lars slipped across

the long top of the cooler, yelping in fright as the whole boat tipped wildly to the side.

"Lars!" Natalie cried out.

But Lars had already plunged overboard into the dark and stormy waters below.

CHAPTER THREE

Lars

Well, this was certainly an adventure.

And Lars knew a thing or two about adventure. Years of living on his own had made him scrappy, teaching him how to keep himself safe while he made daring late-night food raids and intrepid escapes from dogcatchers and dogs alike. Lars may not have known who his mother or father were, or where his next meal was coming from, but he certainly knew how to take care of himself.

And to be clear, Lars *certainly* knew how to swim. He could tell the Praters had been worried about whether or not he could handle himself in the water, but really, would he have gotten on a boat if he *couldn't* swim like a pro? He loved that Natalie girl—who wouldn't?—and after one short week he felt ready to follow her just about anywhere. But he wasn't a dummy. He wouldn't have come out here today if he didn't think he could handle it.

Still, even he had to admit that this was sort of asking a lot.

The moment he stepped into the ocean, he went under. It wasn't even a matter of how hard he could paddle; the surface of the water was rising and falling too fast for him to get an immediate handle on anything, let alone keep his nose above water.

By the time he'd kicked his way back up to the surface, the current had already pulled him yards away from the boat. On the one paw, Lars supposed that was better than getting tangled up in the fishing nets that the Praters had yet to take in. But on the other paw, there was no way Natalie or her dad would be able to see Lars from this far out. It was only a few yards, but in Lars's experience, human eyesight wasn't exactly great, and the darkness and chaos of the storm certainly wasn't helping.

He heard Natalie shout, "Lars! Lars, where are you?!"

Human senses might not have been worth much, but Lars's canine senses were working just fine, and even over the rushing water, he could hear Natalie screaming herself hoarse from the edge of the boat. The sound broke his heart. *I'm here!* he wanted to yell. *I'm okay!* But opening his mouth to bark would have meant risking swallowing seawater.

And if he didn't paddle hard, he wouldn't be okay for much longer. He kicked off toward the boat, determined to make it back safely. It wasn't just for his own sake that he was swimming; it was for Natalie's. And, okay, her father was pretty great, too, and a really reliable friend when you wanted some fish. But Natalie . . . Natalie was special.

Lars had seen a lot of the world, and he had met a lot of people, and the one thing he knew about people was that they were full of surprises. Sometimes they were bad surprises, like when shopkeepers yelled at him, or when kids tried to pull on his whiskers. But way more often than not, they were good surprises. A gift of food here, a belly rub there. It all added up to make Lars believe that everyone had the ability to surprise you for the better, and he had decided long ago to treat them as such. Every human he met, he fell in love with, and stayed there unless they demonstrated that he should do otherwise.

But no human had ever surprised him quite as delightfully as Natalie Prater. From the moment they'd met, she'd treated him the way he treated everyone else: like an instant friend. She'd taken him home, fed him, let him sleep where it was warm, and then—and this was the really amazing bit—she'd fed him *again*. And even after Mr. Prater had said they couldn't keep him, she'd spent all week finding him and giving him food she'd snuck out of school. The best part about the food Natalie brought, other than the fact that it was food, was the way it always smelled slightly like her. Lars had met a lot of humans Natalie's age who put on strong perfumes or deodorants that overwhelmed his sensitive canine nose. But Natalie just smelled clean, with a little bit of earth and a little bit of sea salt and a whole lot of love. Dogs could smell human emotions, and any dog that got near Natalie could smell that this girl had more love than she knew what to do with.

When you met a girl like that, you did anything she asked, including hiding in coolers that smelled like fish for half an hour so you could surprise her father on his fishing boat. And when you fell off that fishing boat, you swam right back toward it, because on that boat was an amazing girl who was looking for you, and letting her down was not an option.

But that was easier said than done. Even now, just as Lars thought he was making progress, he felt another wave pull him backward. It wasn't fair. If these waves were moving him back, they should have been moving the boat back toward him, too. But the ocean didn't care about what was fair, and in any case, a scrawny mutt was a lot easier to toss around than a sturdy fishing boat.

"Lars!"

No excuses, Lars thought. *Natalie needs you.* And he swam harder. And the waves came harder still.

Okay. So this adventure was a bit more difficult

than some of the ones he'd had before. And it didn't help that the rain kept getting in his eyes, and the water out here was really cold, and although he couldn't really afford to think like this, he was definitely starting to get tired.

Be tired later, Lars thought. *Swim now!*

But it was no use. The harder he fought, the more tired he got, and the ocean wasn't tired at all. By now, Natalie's cries were getting fainter. Were they moving farther away? Or was he? If only this rain would let up so he could just *see* something—

Just then, Lars saw something. And he wished he hadn't.

There, cutting through the water a few yards in front of him, was a fin. A gray fin, moving through the water like a knife and then disappearing again, so quick and so camouflaged in the gray-blue ocean that Lars might have imagined it. But his canine eyes wouldn't lie, and Lars had spent enough days begging on enough beaches to know what a fin like that meant:

A shark.

If he hadn't already been neck-deep in freezing-cold

water, Lars would have shuddered. Whereas just a second ago, he'd been this close to giving up, now he knew he *had* to make it back to the *Maria P.* He would *not* be shark bait.

But he might not have much of a choice. The *Maria P.* was officially nowhere to be found at this point, and even his amazing canine sense of direction couldn't help him out of this mess. All he could smell was salt water, and as the fin sliced up the water again, closer this time, he smelled something else—the familiar smell of . . .

Wait. That wasn't shark. Lars never forgot a smell, and he'd smelled shark before; this was something else.

Yeah, he thought wryly. *A different kind of shark. There's more than one type, you know.*

Well, it didn't matter, anyway. That last burst of adrenaline he'd just gotten was already wearing off, leaving him even more tired than he'd been before. First his tail stopped beating in the water, then his legs slowly, slowly began to stop kicking. As long as there was air in his lungs, Lars knew he would float.

But as for paddling or swimming or doing anything else that might get him back to that boat, he was done. Just like the waves crashing around him, this adventure had finally put Lars in over his head. The only thing that would get him out of this now was a miracle.

And then there was the fin again, barely two feet away now. It was so close this time that Lars could hear the sound it made when it emerged from the water—a sound he'd never heard any shark make before.

Puff!

And then, just as Lars's legs gave out completely, something rose beneath him, pushing him up and out of the water with ease.

And Lars got his miracle.

CHAPTER FOUR

Bangor

Bangor had been in the south for less than a day, and it had already been the most exciting day of his entire life.

The drowned canyons of the Atlantic Ocean rolled away to his left as he swam down the very edge of the coastal shelf. To his right, crabs scuttled up the slow slope to the shoreline, snapping at starfish and the occasional lobster. Bangor still hoped to find his family, but the warmer water and the wildlife kept him plenty entertained in the meantime. And the changes in the water brought on by the weather meant the fish were out in force today, which basically gave Bangor access to an all-you-can-eat buffet as he kept just in front of the storm.

But he was also pretty sick of that darn storm. It seemed to be following him. No matter how far he swam, he could feel it closing in on his tail fin every time he tried to slow down and appreciate his surroundings. The storm had to die down eventually, but for now, it felt like he was being chased farther and farther down the coast.

But if the storm was driving him this far down south, was it driving his pod in the same direction? Or were they somewhere on the other side of the maelstrom, having already weathered it out, waiting for him to return to them?

Bangor was looking for something to distract him from these questions, and after swimming for almost the entire day, he finally found just the distraction he was looking for—lights, and lots of them. He'd heard about these stretches of coast from the porpoises that had passed through his home growing up. These were the spots where the ships went when they returned to shore, where the humans made their homes on the land. But based on the lights he was seeing when he surfaced to breathe, these weren't half as big as the scary ships that had separated him from his family. These ships were smaller, and bobbed all together like a flock of very odd and outsized seabirds. Bangor found himself wishing that he could go and check the boats out up close.

Well? What's stopping you? he thought.

It was a fair question. There was no one around to tell him not to—no Belfast to tease him, or Kittery to tell him it was too dangerous.

But Bangor kind of wished there was.

Pushing that thought aside, he made his way into the cove whose shore the lights were scattered across. The rain was already picking up, and he figured he would swim up, get a good look, and then swim out again. But he hadn't gone too far at all before he encountered something: one of the boats, farther out in the cove than any of the others, surrounded beneath the water by delicious fish. Bangor had already had a pretty good day of eating, though, so he hung back, keeping a wide perimeter around the boat as he swam a few curious laps around it. He wasn't sure how stealthy he should be about coming up for air—what would the humans do if they noticed him?—but after a while, it became apparent that they weren't going to notice him at all. They must have been busy with something else. Maybe it had to do with all those fish.

Which, come to think of it, maybe Bangor *was* getting kind of hungry again, and all that food was just sitting there. He made his way closer to the boat, and—

Yikes. Bangor noticed just in time why none of the fish were swimming away from the boat. They couldn't. They were all pressing against a barrier so thin that even Bangor's echolocation had had trouble noticing it. This was something else he'd heard about, not just from wandering porpoises but from his own mother: fishing nets. The human tool that was dangerous not just for fish but for any creature of the sea.

There went one of the nets now, rising up out of the water and onto the boat. Bangor respected a healthy appetite for fish as much as the next porpoise. He'd grown up watching Uncle York in action, and even four nets full of fish seemed normal compared to some of the hauls he'd seen that guzzler take in. But Bangor had no interest in being part of anyone's haul, and anyway, the waves were really starting to pick up in the cove. This was probably his cue to get back out into the open water and move south again.

Or maybe north. Maybe this brush with danger was a sign that he really did need his pod to watch over him. Maybe he should be more worried about finding his family than—

Splash!

Over by the boat, something had fallen into the water—something large enough that Bangor heard it instantly. He turned back to the boat, clicking curiously to see what it was. Had a human dived into the waves?

No, it wasn't a human. Too many legs, and a thrashing tail, to boot. But it wasn't anything Bangor had seen before, either. The closest thing he could think of was the leatherback turtles he had seen sometimes, migrating through the northern Atlantic. This thing was sort of like those, but less round, and with no shell, and fur all over its body. It was some kind of . . . fur turtle.

But based on how the fur turtle was desperately treading water, he and Bangor had something in common that real turtles didn't: They both needed to be above water to breathe. And it seemed like the fur turtle needed to do it a lot more frequently than Bangor did. Like, all the time, in fact. And with each passing wave that pulled the creature backward and down, it seemed like it was having a harder and harder time getting the air it required.

On some level, Bangor knew this wasn't his problem. This was a dangerous cove, full of humans and ships and nets and lashing waves. But as those waves pulled at the fur turtle, he was reminded of Bristol, tossed about by the storm, crying out for help from her loved ones. And the farther the fur turtle got from the spot where he'd entered the water, the harder he paddled, trying to be reunited with the boat he'd fallen off. His family must have been on that boat, and now he was separated from his family. That didn't just remind Bangor of Bristol; it reminded Bangor of himself.

Bangor had to help. The only problem was, he wasn't sure exactly *how* to help. While he tried to think of exactly what he would do, he closed in and circled the fur turtle cautiously, puffing occasionally as he did so. By drawing in slowly, he wanted to send a message: *It's okay. I'm not a threat. Let's just be smart about this and figure it out together.*

The fur turtle evidently saw Bangor's message loud and clear, and then completely failed to understand it. The moment he noticed Bangor was there, he surged through the water, paddling twice as hard as before in his efforts to get away. But there was no real direction for the creature to go—frankly, he didn't seem able to swim as well as a turtle at all—and he seemed to be growing tired quickly. Too tired. If Bangor didn't intervene soon, he got the sense that this poor creature's head wouldn't be staying above the water much longer.

Right. That settled it. Bangor took one more breath, then submerged himself below the waves, positioning himself carefully so that he was right under the fur turtle, and a little bit behind. Gently but firmly, he rose up under the poor animal, and—success!—lifted him right out of the water.

At first he could feel the fur turtle, or whatever it was, panicking, scrabbling at the slick surface of Bangor's back. But every time it seemed like he was in danger of falling off, or being pushed off by a wave, Bangor patiently and precisely adjusted his balance. Soon the animal was perched perfectly on top of him; his back was pressed up against Bangor's dorsal fin, his front legs were resting on either side of Bangor's blowhole, and his head was fully—and thankfully—up and out of the water.

"*Eee-eee-eee,*" Bangor cried. Hopefully, the fur turtle would get the message better this time: *Don't. Move. A. Muscle.*

Some swift echolocation showed him that the ocean floor dropped out and away in front of him, meaning he did *not* want to go there. He turned himself around, taking care not to drop his new friend, and began the journey up the shallows to the shore.

49

Bangor had never tried swimming with anything on top of him before, and certainly never through such stormy waters. He found himself straining muscles he never even knew he had, and what should have been a short journey quickly began to feel like an excruciatingly long one. And if he was having a tough time, it wasn't half as bad as what the creature on his back seemed to be experiencing. For an animal Bangor had met in the water, the fur turtle didn't seem to be well designed for aquatic life at all. It was a lot of pressure to put on one porpoise, and he almost lost his patience entirely when the creature, in a moment of fear, dug his claws into Bangor's back. *Ouch!* What kind of jerk hurt the animal that was saving him?

But then he thought of Bristol again, and his whole family, and what he would say if—*when*—he met them again. When they were back together, Bangor wanted to be proud of what he'd done while they were gone. And letting this poor, defenseless creature fall into the water, no matter how sharp his claws were, would not have made Bangor proud at all.

So he puffed impatiently, knowing that the air would shoot right into the fur turtle's face: *Hey, pal. Lay off.*

His passenger must have gotten the message this time, because he instantly eased up on Bangor's back.

"Eee-eee-ee-ee-e-e-e!" Bangor squeaked his approval.

"Rrff!" responded the fur turtle.

So that was what they sounded like. Kind of like a seal, but less obnoxious. Maybe Bangor's new friend wasn't such a jerk after all.

Now that Bangor was getting better at it, keeping the fur turtle balanced on his back felt almost like a game. If they hadn't met in such crazy conditions, Bangor might have liked to do this just for the fun of it, the way he liked breathing or exploring. And now that the rain was even letting up a little, maybe the worst of the storm had finally passed.

The water was getting shallower and shallower, and they were almost at the shoreline. With a rising sense of pride, Bangor prepared himself for the moment he would drop off his passenger, and then . . .

What? Bangor didn't know. He'd never prepared

for something like this before. He'd never even imagined something like this before.

And as the edge of the beach approached, Bangor couldn't help but wonder if the most exciting day of his life so far might just become more exciting still.

CHAPTER FIVE

Natalie

This was quite possibly the worst day of Natalie's life.

The day her parents had told her they were divorcing had been pretty bad, to be sure, but at least that hadn't been her fault. A very high number of people had gone very far out of their way to assure Natalie that absolutely none of that was her fault. But this? This was entirely because of her. And there was nothing she could do. But she'd be darned if she wouldn't try and do something anyway.

"Lars!" she screamed again, leaning as far as she dared over the back of the boat. *"Lars, where are you?!"*

She'd screamed herself hoarse from every side of the deck. Behind her, Natalie's father was doing his part, turning on all of the *Maria P.*'s lights and even breaking out the emergency flashlights from their compartment in the wheelhouse. But Natalie felt a very real fear that it was all in vain. Lars had vanished from sight almost instantly after falling into the water, and they hadn't seen hide nor hair of him since. For all she knew, he'd gone under the first time and never come back up.

She'd taken a dog out on the ocean, and she hadn't even known if he could swim. Nobody could tell her this wasn't her fault. Natalie turned to face her father, who was dutifully sweeping his flashlight across the water and squinting as hard as he could.

"We have to do something, Dad!" she yelled. "We have to go in there and look for him!"

"No way." Her father looked like she'd suggested lighting the boat on fire. "Absolutely not."

"But, *Dad*," Natalie cried, and she didn't even care that she was "But, *Dad*"-ing again. "Lars needs us!"

She grabbed the railing with both her hands and looked out at the water, trying to steel herself mentally for what she wanted to do. It was cold down there, and dangerous, but if she had a chance of finding Lars, she was ready to go in.

As it turned out, she wouldn't get that chance. The moment Mr. Prater saw what his daughter was doing, he threw his flashlight to the ground, grabbed Natalie by both shoulders, and looked her square in the eye.

"Honey, listen to me. Please," Mr. Prater said. "He hasn't even been in the water for two whole minutes, and we already have no idea where he is. Do you think I'm going to let my own daughter go in there? I refuse to lose both of you. Your safety is more important to me than anything—*anything*—else. You cannot go in that water."

His tone was so urgent, so emotional, that even in this moment of crisis, Natalie was taken by surprise.

"O-okay," she said. "But we have to find him!"

Her father nodded. "We'll do our best. Now, help me get these nets up, and then we can look."

In all the commotion, Natalie had totally forgotten about the two starboard nets that were still in the water. They jumped to it, pulling the remaining hauls in what Natalie thought had to be the fastest fish collection she'd ever seen in her life. Then her father started the boat back up and circled it around as slowly as possible. Natalie picked up both flashlights and stood on the deck, scanning every inch of the water. The whole time, she yelled as hard as she could, until she barely had a voice, until they were almost back to shore, until she knew in her heart there was no way Lars would respond. By the time they'd returned to port, Natalie's face was soaked in stinging salt water, and she knew that it wasn't just because of the waves.

A small wooden drawbridge spanned the entrance to the port. To enter or exit, someone had to hold down a big red button until the bridge went all the way up. It was supposed to be the harbormaster's job, but he wasn't around tonight; he must have figured nobody would be crazy enough to go out in this weather. Normally, when the harbormaster was off duty, Natalie loved hopping out of the boat to operate the drawbridge herself. Who wouldn't love a chance to hit an actual big red button? But now, Mr. Prater eyed her nervously.

"If you want," he began, "I can—"

But Natalie was already headed for the edge of the boat. She figured she could use the distraction. She was careful not to slip on the rain-slicked dock, but as she ran up the wooden steps to the drawbridge control panel, she was surprised by how much things had cleared up by now compared to just a few minutes ago. The storm must have been calming down. By the time she got to the button, the rain had slowed to the lightest of drizzles, and she had a clearer view of her surroundings—all the boats in the harbor to one side and the sandy beach to the other.

Just then, she heard a strange sound emanating from somewhere within the surf, just before the whole bridge went up in a symphony of creaks and groans.

Puff!

What was that? As the drawbridge rose, Natalie's eyes scanned the shore, trying to find the source of the noise. She didn't see any people on the beach. All she saw was—

"Natalie!" her father yelled a minute later, as the *Maria P.* passed under the drawbridge and into port. "Natalie, you have to lower the bridge again!"

But Natalie was no longer at the button. She had already dashed down the staircase, shoes thunking on every wooden step; and then she was leaping from the boardwalk to the beach path; and then she was pounding across the wet sand, all thoughts of anything else totally forgotten.

"Lars!" she yelled. "Lars, you made it!"

"Wroof! Wroof!" There, bouncing happily on the beach, was Lars. He jumped up, putting his two front paws on Natalie's shoulders and licking her face, and Natalie wrapped him in a tight hug, squeezing him against the squishy surface of her life jacket. Lars looked like he'd just emerged from a laundry machine's spin cycle—and he smelled like he really needed a laundry machine's spin cycle. But to Natalie, he was the most beautiful thing she'd ever seen.

"Don't you *ever* scare me like that again!" She let Lars drop back down to all fours, where he panted happily up at her and then shook out his fur. From the looks of his matted coat, it was the seventh or eighth time he'd done it, and he still wasn't getting any less wet.

"Natalie!" That was her father, panting as he ran up behind her. "I tied off as fast as I could. Nat, what's going on?"

Natalie wasn't even sure how to answer. How could she explain this? She knelt down and scratched Lars right behind both of his ears, just the way he liked it.

"How did you get back here?" she asked him, studying his face for a clue. "How did you possibly survive?"

Lars just smiled at her and licked her nose again. As answers went, it was cute, but not very helpful.

Puff!

There was that noise again, coming from somewhere past the waterline. As her father put his hands on his hips and stared down at Lars, Natalie slowly stood up and studied the surf.

Puff! Puff! Pufffftttt!

If Natalie didn't know better, she'd say the sound was getting impatient with her. This time, her father heard it, too, and he turned to look where Natalie was looking.

"What in the—" he began, and then, "Oh, *wow*."

There, gazing at them from just above the water, its dark gray back blending almost entirely into the cold April tide, was—

"A dolphin!" Natalie cried in amazement.

"No," her father said, just as amazed. "Look at the rounded snout. It's a harbor porpoise. They're much shyer than dolphins. I've never seen one this up close for so long."

As if grateful to finally be recognized, the porpoise rolled slightly to one side and then the other, his pectoral fins wiggling out of the water one at a time.

"He's waving!" Natalie cried, delighted. Meanwhile, her father was looking slowly from the porpoise, to Lars, and then back to the porpoise again.

"I don't believe it..." he said in quiet astonishment.

But Natalie was already two steps ahead of him, and she absolutely believed it.

"Did you rescue our dog?" she asked the porpoise. "Did you bring him back to shore?"

The porpoise puffed one more time, and then squeaked out a chipper reply.

"Rreee!"

Natalie wanted to say something back, but she was interrupted.

"Rrff!" Lars barked.

At the sound of the porpoise's voice, Lars had stood up and dashed, barking, into the surf.

"They're *talking*!" Natalie could barely keep up with all the amazing things that were happening. This had gone from the worst day of her life to the best so fast that she hadn't even had time to question it. And now, as the last of the rain cleared away and the moon began to poke out of the clouds, she realized just how late it was, and how much she'd been through today, and just how very, *very* tired she had become all of a sudden.

As if on cue, the porpoise squeaked one last time at Lars, gave one last roll-wiggle of its fins, and then disappeared back into the water. The last thing they saw was its tail, slapping against the surf, and then it was gone, like it had never been there at all.

Except for the dripping-wet dog it had deposited on the side of the shore.

"Wait!" Natalie yelled. "I didn't even get to say thank you." But the sentence got quieter as she said it, her throat finally reminding her that it had been yelling in the rain for almost thirty straight minutes. Just as she began to feel faint, Natalie felt her father's arm wrap around her side, holding her up.

"If I see him when I'm out there," he said softly, "I'll tell him thank you from all of us. Now, come on. It's been a long day. Let's all go home."

For once, Natalie was too tired to argue. She just let her father guide her back toward their shack, looking down at her feet, making sure one went in front of the other, even as Lars darted around her heels with as much energy as ever. As she stumbled through their front door and down the hall to her room, something registered in the fog of Natalie's tired mind: Mr. Prater had let Lars come back to the shack with them.

And when she'd said "our dog" back on the beach, he hadn't corrected her.

As she settled into her bed just a few minutes later,

Natalie came to a decision. She *had* to find that porpoise again. Because in the days to come, she felt she would have a *lot* to thank him for.

Then Natalie closed her eyes, and the whole world went dark.

CHAPTER SIX

Lars

The whole world was dark. But luckily, dogs had excellent night vision. Lars padded through the Prater household as quietly as he could, trying to find a good place to sleep. He would have loved nothing more than to curl up in bed with Natalie, but he knew there were a few reasons that he shouldn't even try that.

First of all, he was already pushing his luck with Mr. Prater by being in the house at all. Just because his overboard adventure had given everyone a scare didn't mean he could suddenly act like royalty.

Second, he smelled like a clump of washed-up seaweed with fur, and he knew it. Humans always thought dogs didn't know how bad they smelled when they were wet, but the exact opposite was true.

Humans only had human noses to work with. They couldn't smell the *half* of it.

And finally, Lars always had trouble sleeping near people, even on the best of nights. He was a very active dreamer, and he'd been woken up lots of times by people complaining that he was softly kicking or barking in his dreams again, chasing squirrels or trying to communicate with very large tennis balls that had somehow learned to talk. Sometimes he got so loud that he woke himself up.

So he set out on his own to find a nice secluded sleeping spot, and after a few minutes, he found one: a corner of the living room with its very own heating vent—the perfect place for a waterlogged dog to curl up and dry off in his dreams. Before he lay down, he did his traditional three turns around his sleeping territory, acclimating to the soft carpet and the gentle hum of the heating vent.

But on his third rotation, something strange happened. The humming from the heating vent was replaced by another sound, one he'd never heard come out of any vent before. It was a distant gurgling. It sounded almost like there was water bubbling in the walls of the house, somewhere in the distant corners of the ventilation shaft.

Lars didn't know as much about human houses as your typical domestic dog, but he knew that there definitely wasn't supposed to be any water back there. Still, the gurgling was getting louder, now almost a full-on rushing sound. A low growl started in the back of Lars's throat, and his ears pointed stiffly backward as the hair rose all along his back. There was something very wrong inside this heating vent— and it was getting closer by the second.

Suddenly, water flooded out of the vent like a gush from a hose, and even though the vent had been warm just a minute ago, the water that was filling up the living room was ice-cold. And it didn't have the fresh taste of human tap water, either; it was salty and brackish, just like seawater. The water Lars had almost drowned in this evening.

The water was everywhere now, and deep—so deep that Lars couldn't touch the ground. The coffee tables and couches floated past him, crashing into one another, adding an extra threat to the situation. Lars whimpered and barked, not even caring anymore if some of the water went down his throat. He had to warn the Praters. He had to make sure what had happened to him didn't happen again, and certainly not to anyone else. He had to make it to land.

But there was no land. Only water and waves and loud crashing sounds, and the return of the hopelessness he'd felt just hours ago.

And then . . . fins. And a flash of gray.

Then Lars was riding high again, perched on top of his porpoise friend, no longer afraid of anything. They did a loop around the living room furniture, and then they were off, leaping over the waves, gleefully squeaking and barking back and forth. And Natalie was there, too, and Mr. Prater, and everyone was safe and happy. But no one was happier than Lars, because he knew that all of these people—and this porpoise—were his friends. Lars had met a lot of nice people in his life, people who he had always had to move on from, or who had moved on from him. But for the first time in his long and lonely life, this stray dog had finally found some nice people who would come back for him and who would lift him up when he was down. He had *real* friends. And he was happy.

Then he woke up.

Oh. Right. Of course.

It had all been a dream. There had never been a scary flooded heating vent. He had never tried to sleep by a heating vent at all. He had curled up outside Natalie's door, as close to her as he could reasonably get without stinking up her room, and within seconds, he'd fallen asleep and launched into one of his crazy dreams. It was a typical Lars dream— the scary kind that involved worrying and growling and things he couldn't control. But it also *wasn't* the typical Lars dream, because even though he was awake now, he could still remember how amazing the end of the dream had been. It had a happy ending. And it wasn't just something Lars had dreamed up. That feeling—that friendship—was real. And all of those friends were close to him now, sleeping peacefully.

Well, not all of them.

Lars closed his eyes and sniffed the air, flaring his ears out for good measure. His supersensitive hearing could easily make out the birdsong beyond the walls of the Prater household. It was already morning, and Lars had dreamed the whole night away. But if he focused even harder, cast his hearing even farther, smelled the air the way only a dog could . . .

There was the rolling of the waves on the beach outside, soothing and gentle compared to last night's frenzied crashing. And somewhere in those waves . . .

Maybe he was imagining it, but didn't it sound like something was splashing and puffing? There was only one way to find out. As Lars rose to his feet, he was gripped with an absolute certainty that he would find out. After all, friends came back for other friends. And he had a friend to find.

CHAPTER SEVEN

Natalie

Natalie was too tired to dream, so from the moment she closed her eyes to the moment she woke up, it felt like no time had passed at all. But she knew that time *had* passed, because when she had gone to bed it had been dark outside, and now morning light was streaming through her window. Also, when she had gone to bed, it had been very quiet in the house, and now a crazed animal was attempting to claw down her door.

"I'm coming! I'm coming! Lars, calm down, I'm coming!" Natalie couldn't help but smile as she got out of bed, putting on her flip-flops and hurrying to open her door. Lars, who had been up on his hind legs scratching away at the door, toppled into the room ungracefully, landing on his back. But even as Natalie laughed and leaned down to give him a belly rub, he was already up off the ground again, running in circles around Natalie's feet.

"What in the world has gotten into you?" she asked. Lars just barked and shot out of her room, trying to round a corner so fast that he skidded on the hallway's hardwood floor and slammed into the wall of the shack. Natalie laughed again, and Lars immediately picked himself up, dusted himself off, and disappeared down the hall.

Well, there was no use standing there. Natalie grabbed her windbreaker off its door hanger and zipped it over her pajama top, and then dashed down the hall after Lars. Already, Lars was at the front door, where he'd resumed his holding pattern of circling around once, jumping up, scratching at the door, falling back down, and circling around again, punctuating the whole looping process with various yips and barks. Natalie had never seen him so agitated, but he didn't seem upset. He seemed more impatient and excited about something.

"Do you need to go outside?" Natalie asked. "Do you have to pee?" That made her think of something: "Wait, hold on, are you even house-trained? We should really figure that out."

But that would have to wait until another day. Lars barked again, and from somewhere in the shack, Mr. Prater yelled, "Natalie, make him be quiet or make him leave!"

Natalie shrugged and looked down at Lars. "You heard the man," she said, opening the door.

It was like releasing a rock from a slingshot. Lars was out the door so fast that Natalie didn't even see his feet touch the ground. She laughed as he shot across the yard, waiting to see what spot he would choose to do his duty.

But Lars didn't choose a spot in the yard. He didn't stay in the yard at all.

"Wait! Lars!" Natalie called out, but it was too late. He shot down the driveway, into the street, and right down the road that would take him through Main Street and back to the beach. Quickly, Natalie kicked off her flip-flops and shoved her feet into her running shoes. She had already lost this dog once in the last twenty-four hours, and she wasn't about to do it again.

"I'll be back soon, Dad, bye!" she yelled.

"Wait, what?" Mr. Prater yelled back, but Natalie was already off.

Lars was fast, but he was new in town, and Natalie knew these streets like she knew the halls of her own home. If Lars stayed on the main road, she knew she could take a shortcut by doubling behind her own house, leaping over the fence in the backyard, and cutting across the yard of—

"Hi, Nancy Jane!" she yelled. Her next-door neighbor was up to her usual Sunday morning routine, painting a tranquil scene of the birds in her backyard. Presumably, she would not include the girl running by at high speed.

"Morning, Natalie!" Nancy Jane yelled back. "Did you get those photos of the storm last night? It looked like a humdinger!"

"I did!" Natalie responded as she hopped over the fence on the other side of Nancy Jane's yard. "If you want to see them, I think I'll be at the beach!" Then she was back on Main Street, and if she looked down the road to her right . . .

There! Lars. He rocketed past a young boy, barely avoiding a collision, much to the delight of the child and the alarm of the mother just behind him. Natalie recognized her as the wife of Mr. Reardon, Ogunquit's best lobsterman and head of the lobsterman's union.

"Sorry, Mrs. Reardon!" Natalie said as she, too, zoomed past the mother and child. Lars crossed a street, narrowly missing a bicycle, and so did Natalie. She chased the dog across the front lawn of Ogunquit Town Hall.

"Hey! Miss Prater!" That was Mayor Maher, returning from the Coveside Café with his morning coffee. "Did you see that stray dog go by just now? I've been trying to find him all week!"

"Yes! No! He's not a stray! He's mine!" Natalie blurted out, and before anyone could contradict her or ask any follow-up questions, she was gone again.

Lars was passing the Coveside Café now, which meant they were getting close to the beach. Natalie had no idea why a dog who had almost drowned just last night would be so eager to return to the scene of the (thankfully-not-a) crime, but she'd be darned if she let him out of her sight. She picked up the pace, almost knocking into a tourist as they left the café, and before long she was practically on Lars's tail. But even though she'd had a good night's sleep, she was getting exhausted, and she felt like she'd run out of steam if they didn't reach the ocean soon.

The buildings of Ogunquit dropped away and Perkins Cove rose up in their place. First came the boats, then the bridge, and then the beach, dazzling blue in the April morning light. Somehow, Lars had already magically cleared the pile of rocks and reeds that separated the road from the beach proper, but Natalie had to scrabble her way down them, taking care not to twist her ankle or fall headfirst into a boulder.

By the time she got down to level land, Lars was splashing happily across the tide, which was almost all the way in. And there, just a small distance from Lars—

Puff!

Natalie gasped as the water broke apart, revealing the porpoise from last night. Moving with surprising grace for something so round and roly-poly, the porpoise breached, disappeared, and then breached again, this time keeping his head poked out of the water, chittering up a storm.

"Ch-ch-ee-ee-chh!"

"Yarp!"

Lars let loose a joyous noise and took the biggest leap Natalie had ever seen him make, falling back into the water with a titanic splash. In return, the porpoise chittered again and smacked his tail against the surface of the water, sending up a splash of his own.

Now, with a rush of astonished delight, Natalie understood why Lars had been in such a hurry to return to the water. He'd wanted to play with the newest visitor to Perkins Cove. And no wonder. Everyone Lars met, he wanted to be friends with. Why should the porpoise who saved his life be any different?

Watching the two animals chatter and frolic, Natalie couldn't imagine a happier moment. Then Lars broke away from the surf, running up to her. He circled her legs twice, shot back toward the water, and paused for the briefest moment to look back at Natalie. *Are you coming, or not?*

Never mind. *This* was her happiest moment.

Natalie kicked off her shoes, glad she hadn't had time to put on any socks to get all sandy, and dropped her phone in her left sneaker. She rolled up her pajama pants, knotting the ends to keep them from getting wet. Then, slowly, tentatively, not wanting to blow this, she made her way into the water.

The morning sand was smooth and dense, and her toes dug in with each footfall, holding firm as the cold water rushed around her ankles. From its spot in the water, the porpoise eyed her warily, and then surged a little closer—but not too close. The water around Natalie was way too shallow for him, anyway. Natalie exhaled deeply and, wondering why she'd even bothered to roll up her pajama pants, stepped farther into the ocean.

Soon the water was up to her waist, and she began to shiver. She considered herself pretty good at swimming in cold water, but April was still a rough time for a morning dip. The best thing to do would be to dunk herself in all at once and get it over with. She took a deep breath, closed her eyes, and plunged in. The shock of the cold water felt like an icy hand squeezing on her lungs, but when she came back up and pushed her wet hair out of her eyes, she was no longer shivering.

And the porpoise was right next to her.

Natalie gasped, and a chill ran up her spine that had nothing to do with the cold. But when the porpoise looked up at her with his deep, black eyes, she knew she had nothing to be afraid of. Up close, his short snout looked as round and huggable as the rest of his body, and his mouth was curved upward in a slight but unmistakable smile.

"Hello," Natalie said. "Thank you for saving my friend."

The porpoise lazily flapped his fluke up and down, and in doing so, inched ever so slightly closer to Natalie in the water: *Hello to you, too.*

Natalie reached out and gently, slowly, rested one

hand on the side of the porpoise's body, and the other in between his eyes.

His skin was smooth and rubbery and barely warmer than the water around it. But Natalie could feel the life inside, the muscles all made for swimming and spinning and leaping and playing. Just a few inches away from her hand, a pectoral fin pierced the water, and Natalie's gaze was caught by an unexpected gleam of silver. She leaned in closely, and the next time the water parted, she saw it: a small metal tag attached to the fold of her new friend's fin.

Natalie had heard of these tags. Marine biologists placed them on dolphins and porpoises when they were young to track their movements as they grew older. When Natalie looked closer, she could even make out a label written on the tag. She leaned in and squinted through the water.

"Bangor," she read aloud at last. Bangor was a city that was certainly big enough to have a marine biology institute, but it was over a hundred miles up the coast. She thought about the long journey this

porpoise must have taken to get here, and let out a low whistle of astonishment.

"Hweeoo."

Natalie's jaw dropped. The porpoise had whistled back.

"Bangor," she said again, and the porpoise turned his head slightly to look up at her.

And then Lars leaped from the shallow end of the surf, belly-flopping into the water and splashing them both.

Joyous chaos broke out. Natalie laughed and splashed Lars back as Bangor dove into the water and then reemerged between Natalie and Lars, puffing water onto both of them and brushing each of them playfully with his fins. As Lars paddled happily in circles around them, Bangor spun around quickly and went back down into the water.

"Wait for me!" Natalie cried, and then she, too, dove underwater. She'd been practicing swimming with her eyes open since she was in elementary school, and now she was glad she had, because when she opened her eyes, she was able to see Bangor swimming rapidly out and down into the water—and then reversing course and returning at an even faster pace than he'd swum away. Natalie had just enough time to push herself back out of the water, and then—

Whoosh! Bangor burst entirely free from the ocean. For a moment, he hung in the air, his body one big arc, droplets of water flying from his back and glittering in the morning light. Then gravity pulled on his heavy porpoise body, and he fell back into the water with the biggest splash any of them had made yet. Natalie laughed, and Lars rolled several feet backward as Bangor poked his head out of the water and chittered sheepishly.

Natalie never wanted this to end.

"Natalie!"

Not knowing what to expect, Natalie turned and saw her father standing on the beach, also wearing his pajamas. He must have followed his daughter to see where she was running in such a hurry. His hands were on his hips, and he was shaking his head and laughing in disbelief—and he wasn't alone. Natalie and Lars's mad dash through town had clearly attracted some attention, and now the people of Ogunquit were flocking to the beach to see what all the commotion was about.

"Look!" someone said. "That dog and that dolphin are playing together!"

"I think that's actually a harbor porpoise," someone responded.

"Isn't that that stray dog?" a woman asked.

"I heard that girl say it was *her* dog."

"Oh, really? And is that *her* porpoise?"

As the crowd grew, Natalie made out some familiar faces. There was Nancy Jane, clasping her hands together and smiling widely as she watched Lars and Bangor swim alongside each other. There was Mrs. Reardon, totally flabbergasted, trying as best as she could to hold on to her young son, Sam, as he yelled, "Let me in, Mommy, I want to go swim with them!"

And there was Mayor Maher, his expression entirely unreadable. He sipped his coffee as he coolly gazed at the dog and porpoise that were even now drawing more and more people to the beach. Something about the mayor's demeanor made Natalie nervous.

But then she saw Nancy Jane talking excitedly to Natalie's father about the best way to paint porpoises, and seeing her like that made Natalie feel happy. Then Bangor puffed and shot past at high speed, doing another loop around Lars before going back under for a few seconds, then reemerging for another incredible jump. And that made Natalie happier still.

And when Bangor splashed back down, Mr. Prater turned to look, laughed, and gave his daughter a big smile and wave. It was the most carefree Natalie had seen him look in months—specifically, in the months since Natalie's mother had moved in with Diver Bob.

And seeing her father that happy? That made Natalie the happiest of all.

CHAPTER EIGHT

Bangor

After all the excitement of last night's storm, Bangor had badly needed to rest, but he had also been much too excited for that. Porpoises didn't sleep well at the best of times. In fact, they didn't really sleep at all, at least not the way most people thought of sleep. Bangor, along with every other porpoise he'd ever met, only rested one half of his brain at a time. The other half stayed alert for any unexpected threats, meaning that harbor porpoises always slept with one eye open—literally.

But that first night after the storm, Bangor truly felt like he was split in two, and not just because he was trying to sleep. As one half of his mind rested, the other half raced, replaying the events of the daring storm rescue over and over again. Then, midway through the night, he put that half of his mind to sleep, and the *other* half raced, thinking about his family and wondering where they might be.

By the morning, when the light began to pierce the now-calm waters of the cove, Bangor knew he had a decision to make. Should he go back out into the ocean to look for his family? Or should he stay here, in case any more exciting adventures cropped up? On the one fin, he couldn't imagine an adventure more exciting than what had happened last night. On the other, just twenty-four hours ago, he could never have imagined an adventure like this at *all*. Who knew what else might await him here with these strange new creatures he'd met?

In the end, it was the thought of those creatures—that little human and that funny fur turtle she had called Lars—that convinced him he had to stay. At the very least, it would only be proper for him to tell them good-bye before he left again.

And almost as soon as Bangor had had that thought, he heard that familiar seal-like barking. It echoed from somewhere far out of the water, but it rapidly came closer, accompanied by a high-pitched human yelling. The sounds grew louder and louder, then climaxed in a tumult of splashing and paws as the fur turtle, Lars, tumbled full tilt into the water.

Bangor's heart swelled. While he'd been thinking of them, they'd been thinking of him! He breached to get a better look at Lars, who was jumping and panting happily. Bangor spun in place to register his pleasure. Lars promptly attempted to do the same thing but got too excited in the rolling tide, tripping over his own large and waterlogged paws. It was funny, and it made Bangor squeak with laughter, and that seemed to make Lars happy.

As they played together, Bangor noticed someone on the beach behind Lars. It was the young girl from the night before, the one who the larger human had called Natalie. She was standing and watching them, as if unsure whether or not to come in. To be honest, Bangor felt a little nervous about her, as well. In his experience, humans, especially the ones with boats, could be dangerous creatures whether they knew it or not, with their loud sounds and invisible fishing nets.

But it was clear from the way she looked at them that she was a big fan of Lars, and Bangor was becoming a big fan of Lars, so they at least had that much in common. And when Lars ran around Natalie's feet to lead her into the water, her care and concern as she approached them were obvious. Bangor was surprised by how comfortable he felt floating as close to her as he reasonably thought he could, and then a little closer still.

He felt one of Natalie's hands come to rest on his side, and the other upon his melon—the part of his head that helped him to echolocate better. Her touch was warm and gentle.

"Bangor," she said aloud.

Then she did something that shocked Bangor: She tried to speak porpoise, whistling a long, low note. It was gibberish in porpoise speak, and it made her sound insane, but mostly Bangor was just impressed that she was trying. It was a good effort, for a human, and he felt that it deserved a response.

"Hweeoo," he whistled politely.

The girl's eyes went wide with surprise.

And then they both got a surprise when Lars jumped, releasing a massive splash and signaling that playtime had truly begun.

As the three of them dipped and dove and laughed and leaped, Bangor was glad he'd stayed. After just a couple days on his own, he'd already managed to meet two souls as goofy and adventurous as he was. And it looked like he was about to meet a lot more.

Then Bangor heard a shout. *"Natalie!"*

There on the beach was the older human from last night. Bangor guessed he was a member of Natalie's pod, and quite possibly the leader. Also on the beach were a number of humans Bangor didn't recognize, and that number was getting bigger. In fact, these were the most humans he'd ever seen in one place, all of them chattering and craning their necks to see what would happen next.

Well, if they wanted a show, Bangor would give them one. He took a deep breath, did a few circles around his new friends to gain speed, and then took another leap out of the water. Harbor porpoises didn't leap like that very often, but Bangor loved it the way he loved everything else about coming to the surface, and even more than that, he loved the applause he got from the humans after he did it. Finally! People who appreciated his cool moves! Maybe humans weren't so bad after all.

But no sooner had he thought that than another man pointed at Natalie and waved her over. Natalie turned to Bangor, gave him one more affectionate pat on the melon, and then made her way back to shore.

Bangor had thought that Natalie's father was the leader of her pod, but based on the way everyone on the beach gave this new man a wide and respectful berth, it seemed, perhaps, he was the real leader of the much larger pod that was this human village. In addition to their echolocation skills, porpoises had excellent hearing, so Bangor was able to hear what the man said to Natalie as she approached him, seawater dripping from her rolled-up clothes.

"Miss Prater, I think you and I have a lot to discuss. You, me, and the whole town. I'll be holding a town meeting as soon as possible, and I'll expect you—and that dog—to be there."

"Yes, Mayor Maher," said Natalie.

And while Bangor couldn't understand what was being said exactly, he could still make out the vibrations of the man's voice, vibrations that did not sound extremely positive. In fact, they sounded very serious, and they made Bangor wonder if maybe not every human was as appreciative and adventurous as his new friends were.

But then Lars paddled up to Bangor, snuffling and snorting against the side of his snout. It tickled, and it made Bangor laugh—*"Ee-ee-ee!"*—and when Bangor made a happy sound, almost everyone on the shore made a happy sound, too.

Worries about town meetings could wait. Swimming back out into the ocean could wait. For now, Bangor had some new friends to play with, and that felt like Bangor's most exciting adventure yet.

CHAPTER NINE

Lars

Mayor Maher set the town meeting for the end of that week, on Friday. For five whole days, it was all anyone in Ogunquit could talk about. Everyone was buzzing about the events of Sunday morning, and Lars, who'd had several dozen dog years in which to perfect the art of eavesdropping, made sure he heard all of it. Each day, while Natalie was at school, Lars lurked around the Coveside Café, slipped himself underfoot outside scuba shops, and, of course, hung around the back doors of restaurant kitchens, waiting for scraps of food and scraps of gossip at the same time.

Lots of people were excited, but the buzz wasn't all positive. That was nothing new for Lars. As a stray, he knew he wasn't always welcome everywhere, even if nice people like Natalie wished he was. But what *was* new was the extra hot topic of debate: the porpoise who had taken up shelter in Perkins Cove. Some people were delighted. Some were concerned or confused. Others who hadn't been there on Sunday didn't even believe it had actually happened, even though Lars had been visiting Bangor at the beach for playtime every morning since Sunday, and could have happily confirmed the whole thing, if anyone cared to listen.

But there wasn't much listening going on in Ogunquit that week, just lots and lots of talking. And at 7:00 p.m. on Friday night, all of those talkers came together under one roof at Ogunquit Town Hall. The voices that had volleyed back and forth all week filled the small room up to the brim, bouncing off the walls with words and worries and many, many opinions. Lars, who had snuck into the meeting between Natalie and Mr. Prater, stayed low to the ground, where he put his paws over his sensitive ears and hoped the humans would quiet down soon.

Mayor Maher cut through the noise with a request for order, which Lars approved of: "Quiet! Please, be quiet!" Then he loudly thwacked a gavel, which Lars wasn't as crazy about.

Even though the mayor wasn't an actual judge, the crowd fell silent almost right away. In a town as small as Ogunquit, everyone knew the mayor. And when everyone knew the mayor and continued to vote for him, it meant people really liked their mayor.

"Shall we take attendance?" Mayor Maher asked.

"Oh, let's just skip it," said Mr. Reardon. "Everyone who's anyone is here."

Mr. Reardon was the head of the local lobsterman's union, and people respected him almost as much as they respected Mayor Maher. Lars could smell it on everyone sitting near him. Mr. Reardon was also correct about the attendance, and Lars could smell that, too. Mr. Reardon's corner of the room was stuffed up with the salty, sweaty smell of sea workers—a group that Mr. Prater perched at the front and center of, with Natalie and Lars by his side. Behind them, in the back right of the room, were the small-business owners and shopkeepers, all dust and wood. In the front left of the room were the retirees and local commerce councilmen, each one smelling musty and old, except for Nancy Jane, who smelled, as always, like paint and café pastries. Lars was a big fan of Nancy Jane. And from the very far back left of the room wafted the unmistakable scent of sunscreen—some hapless tourists who had visited Ogunquit in the off-season and wandered into the only entertainment they could find on a small-town Friday night.

There were a lot of people all there to discuss one thing: Lars and his new friend, the porpoise, and what was to be done about either of them—or if anything should be done at all.

Okay, so maybe that was more than one thing. Lars was getting a little bit stressed. And although Natalie was trying not to show it, she was clearly stressed, as well. She couldn't stop tapping her foot, which was very hard for Lars not to notice, since his head was lying directly next to it.

"Very well, then," Mayor Maher said. "Let's begin the meeting. We all know why we're here today. After the events of this past Sunday—"

"I heard it didn't even happen!" one of the lobster-men huffed.

"It did too!" said little Sam Reardon. "I saw it."

"Please, please!" The mayor raised his hands, but to Lars's immense relief, he did not bang the gavel again. "Clearly, this subject has riled a lot of us up. Which is exactly why we're here to discuss it."

"What's to discuss?" Natalie blurted out. Everyone in the room who'd been pretending not to look at her, the cause of all the commotion, now gave up and turned their attention directly on her. Her cheeks flushed red, but when she continued speaking, her voice didn't waver, and Lars couldn't have been prouder.

"Lars is a good dog," Natalie went on, "and Bangor's an extremely friendly porpoise. They make each other happy, and that makes me—makes *all* of us—happy. I don't see why there's a problem."

"Yeah!" Sam Reardon yelled again. "I want to go swim with the doggy and the dolphin!"

"It's a harbor porpoise," said Nancy Jane.

"That's the problem right there," Mayor Maher said.

"The problem is that it's a porpoise?" Mr. Prater asked.

"No." The mayor waved his gavel at Sam. "The problem is that children, and other people, will want to go out in the cove and swim with an unsupervised wild animal—with *two* unsupervised wild animals."

"Lars isn't—" Natalie began, but the mayor was on a roll.

"Even if one or both of those animals are safe— and that's two big *ifs*," he began, "Perkins Cove is *not*. It's a commercial waterway with high boat traffic and an unpatrolled beach with no lifeguard budget, even in the off-season. Children could get hurt. The animals themselves could get hurt. Without a way to regulate things, the whole situation is risky."

"You can't *regulate* a living creature," said Nancy Jane.

The mayor stumbled mid-speech. "M-Ms. Renaud, please—"

"Please yourself, Mayor," Nancy Jane said. "And call me Nancy Jane; I've known you since grade school."

Now it was the mayor's turn to blush. He seemed unable to formulate a response.

"He's right." Another fisherman, Mr. Grundy, was more than happy to take over. "The whole thing is dangerous. Half of us have already accidentally caught dolphins in our nets when we're out on the water, and it's not good for anyone. Now we have to worry about a dolphin under our drawbridge?"

"I thought it was a harbor porpoise," said a tourist from the back.

"Pingers!" Natalie said. Once again, everyone looked at her, but this time with a sense of confusion.

"They're acoustic alarms," she explained, "that fishermen can put on their nets. They make sounds that warn dolphins and porpoises not to come too close so that they don't get stuck with all the fish. If you had those on your boats, you wouldn't have to worry!"

The crowd murmured among themselves, and Natalie sat back, radiating pride. Lars was proud, too. He'd followed her to and from the Ogunquit Public Library that week, watching her furiously research marine safety.

"Where are we gonna get the budget for these acoustic doohickeys?" Mr. Grundy cut in.

"They'll pay for themselves!" Natalie said. "You said it yourself—you've all suffered from this problem before. Once you get these, no more problems, and lots more fish!"

"Natalie brings up an excellent point," a new voice interjected. "Money."

Even though the voice was agreeing with Natalie, Lars noticed something strange happen to Natalie: She tensed up, her pride and satisfaction evaporating instantly. Her hand, which had been lightly scratching behind Lars's ears—a recent development Lars had been very pleased with—now froze on top of Lars's neck.

From back in the small-business corner, a heavy-set man with curly hair and loud Hawaiian-print clothing stood up. As he spoke, he gestured with his hands, and waves of smell radiated off them—crab and turtle and all kinds of exotic marine life Lars had never even met before. The rest of the man's body smelled of neoprene, the material they used to make wet suits.

"Hello, everyone," he said. "Diver Bob here."

"We know who you are, Bob," the mayor said. Chuckles broke out around the room. Clearly, people were used to this colorful character. But Natalie didn't chuckle at all. In fact, her grip on the back of Lars's neck tightened ever so slightly.

"Well, if you all know who I am," Diver Bob said, "then you all know that I love marine life of any and every kind. And so do our tourists! It's one of the things that keeps people coming back here year after year. And when people find out we have our very own harbor porpoise, they'll be flocking in every weekend!" He turned to the innkeepers and restaurant owners around him. "How is this not a win for everyone?"

"Because they're not here *now*," said Mr. Reardon. "It's April, and it's still cold outside. It'll be weeks before anyone with real money wants to freeze in the water with a lost porpoise." He turned in his seat to look at the couple of tourists in the back of the room. "No offense," he said.

"All the more reason to keep the porpoise around until then." This came from a woman who stood up next to Diver Bob—a woman who made Lars's nostrils flare. She smelled *exactly* like Natalie, or at least very, very close. There was just a little less of the saltwater scent to her, and a little more *eau de* Diver Bob. But she also had Natalie's wavy dirty-blonde hair and defined jaw. Was that why she was looking at Natalie now, her eyes so full of concern? And if so, why were Natalie's own eyes glued to the floor, her cheeks burning even brighter than before?

"Hear, hear." Now Nancy Jane was standing, and Natalie exhaled, loosening her grip on Lars's neck. She was clearly glad the conversation had shifted to another corner of the room.

"I think these animals and their friendship can only be good for our town," Nancy Jane continued. "They're testaments to the love and closeness of our community, as exemplified by our dear young Miss Prater, who brought our attention to them in the first place. If we're worried about one of them popping up where they shouldn't be, then surely the answer is to give them even more attention, so that we always know where they are. I know I'd love to paint them. They're just the splash of bright color I've been looking for in this town."

"Everyone loves your paintings, Nancy Jane," Mr. Reardon said. "But a lot of us in Ogunquit, we don't sell paintings. We sell food, and we get that food from the water. If something gets in the way of that, we have no food. And then we can't sell the food, and then we don't have any money to buy any of the food that we never even got. And that's all *before* we even get to talking about that mangy mutt. Bad enough to have to worry about a fish-stealing dog on land. Now we have one messing around in the water, as well?"

Lars perked up at that last part. He didn't always have time to wash his coat, but *mangy*? There was no need for language like that.

"No matter what," Mr. Reardon concluded, "I think I speak for all of us in the unions when I say that *something* has to be done." Then he looked over at the

Praters, his gaze landing particularly on Natalie's father. "Well," he said, "maybe not quite all of us."

Mr. Prater blushed, but just like Natalie, he didn't let the goading comment get to him. Instead he rose and spoke slowly and calmly. Lars saw now where Natalie got her backbone from.

"It's amazing that so many people in this town are so concerned with what a dog and a porpoise are doing down at the beach," he said. "It's odd, but it's good. Hearing everyone so concerned shows we care about our town, and about one another. And when we care about people, we worry about them." He shot a meaningful look at Natalie, who tried to act like she hadn't seen it.

The townspeople remained silent, looking at Mr. Prater expectantly.

"But are we sure we're not worrying too much?" Mr. Prater continued. "It's been a week, and nothing bad has happened so far. What if we're just imagining bad things that *might* happen, instead of things that *will* happen? When my daughter brought home a stray dog to our house, I imagined lots of bad things might happen. What I got instead was a new friend for her—for both of us. At a time when we really needed one."

He glanced back over his shoulder for the briefest of seconds, flicking his gaze toward the strange woman next to Diver Bob. Lars decided he was officially going to have to work even harder on his eavesdropping abilities if he wanted to figure out what was going on there.

"So let's stay concerned," Mr. Prater said. "But let's not give in to worry. Maybe there's a way to get the porpoise to move half a mile up the beach, so he's not right in the cove. Maybe we can apply for a grant for these pingers. Let's give ourselves some time to figure it out, rather than rush to a ruling at one town meeting. Does that sound fair?"

The whole crowd muttered and nodded, but Mr. Prater wasn't looking at the whole crowd. He was looking first at Mr. Reardon, and then up at Mayor Maher.

The mayor looked back at Mr. Prater, looked up at the ceiling, and then sighed and nodded.

"Of course that's fair," he said. "But I'll be

checking in personally with you, Mr. Prater, so get thinking quick. In the meantime, we'll hold off on taking any drastic action."

Natalie gasped with joy, and the buzz in the room began to build as people either celebrated or expressed their doubts. Sensing that the meeting was swiftly coming to an end, Mayor Maher raised his gavel one last time and pointed it directly at Lars.

"And make sure that dog wears a leash around town," he said. "At all times!"

Wait, what? Lars looked up at Natalie's face, hoping she wouldn't take that crazy suggestion seriously. But she was already facing away from him, looking back at Diver Bob and the woman who smelled like her.

Mayor Maher brought the gavel down one last time—*thwack!*—and Lars jumped in the air as the meeting adjourned.

CHAPTER TEN

Natalie

"I don't think he likes the leash very much," Natalie said.

It was Sunday, two days since the meeting, and Natalie and her father were sitting at the kitchen table, staring down at Lars, who stared up at them from the floor. Normally, he'd have been up on Natalie's lap, angling for some leftover omelet, but he seemed to have been thrown for a loop by the brown strap that had just been wrapped around his neck.

"*I* don't like the leash very much," Natalie's father said. "Do you know how much it costs to find a waterproof leash for a dog who you know is going to be in the water a lot?"

Natalie saw an opening. "In that case, let's return it and—"

"*But*," her father interrupted. "Since Mayor Maher is being so nice about Lars, it'd be nice of us to play very squarely by his rules until we get this whole animal situation figured out."

Natalie sighed, but in her heart, she knew he was right. The leash clearly made both her and Lars uncomfortable, but it was a start. Just like getting her father to let Lars sit under the table was a start toward convincing him to let her keep Lars. Not that she would say that last part out loud just yet. She didn't want to jinx anything.

"Speaking of getting things figured out," Mr. Prater said, standing up to clear the plates from the table, "I have to head out. Some people are getting together to discuss what might be done about relocating Bangor—"

"I thought you wanted him to stay?"

"—to a *safer part of the beach*," Mr. Prater finished quickly. "Still in Ogunquit. This is a meeting of like-minded people, Natalie."

That made Natalie so excited that she got up to

help with the cleaning herself. "Can I come?" she asked, depositing some dishes next to her father at the sink.

Her father froze. "Um," he said, looking at the dishes Natalie had stacked up like they were suddenly the most interesting thing in the world. "You might not want to—that is, this is a meeting for adults, and . . ."

Natalie recognized that voice. That was the voice her father used when he was trying but failing to explain something serious to his daughter. And one person inspired that voice more than anyone else.

"Are you meeting *Mom*?" Natalie cried out, so loud that Lars leaped up from the floor and bonked his head under the table.

"You heard her at the meeting," Mr. Prater said, finally turning to face Natalie. "She wants to help. She and . . . and . . ."

"And *Diver Bob*?!" Natalie threw her hands in the air. "You can't even say his name!"

"Because I know you'll react like this!" her father responded. "You know, your mother told me she tried to talk to you after the meeting."

It was true. As the townspeople had filed out of Ogunquit Town Hall, giving Natalie and Lars either quick smiles or discouraging scowls, Natalie had felt a tap on her shoulder. She'd turned around to see her mother, her face the picture of concern.

"Natalie," she'd said. "I just wanted to say—"

"Uh, Lars has to pee," Natalie had blurted. And she'd run from the room, followed by a confused but loyal Lars.

"I just don't see why they have to be involved," Natalie said now. "I think we can figure things out on our own."

Her father closed his eyes, took a deep breath, and held it for several moments. When he had exhaled, he opened his eyes again, and they looked different from before—less defensive, more forgiving. This annoyed Natalie, who did not feel she had done anything she needed to be forgiven for.

"Everyone needs help sometimes," he said. "You should know that better than anyone, since you're always going out of your way to help people. And porpoises. And even smelly stray dogs."

Natalie looked down at Lars, who had wandered into the kitchen, in case any omelet bits were going to get dropped during all the yelling. His leash trailed limply on the floor behind him.

"I guess," she said. "I just think if you're going to help someone"—she looked at the fridge, at the spot where a photo of the three of them used to be—"you shouldn't leave them."

She looked back up at her father, and this time, he didn't seem to have an answer.

Just then, there was a knock on the front door.

It was a strange knock, because it came from the bottom half of the door, as if someone very short wanted to come inside. Sure enough, when Natalie's father opened the door, he had to look down to see who was knocking. It was little Sam Reardon, wearing a ridiculously puffy life jacket. Mrs. Reardon stood behind him on the Praters' porch, smiling sheepishly.

"Hello, Natalie," she said. "Jim." She nodded at Natalie's father. "I was wondering if—"

"Bangor is back at the beach and I wanna go talk to him before he goes away now, now, *now*!" Sam burst in, waving his arms up and down as much as the life jacket would allow. Mr. Prater laughed, and despite herself, Natalie giggled.

"I was at the market when someone said the porpoise was back," Mrs. Reardon explained wearily. "Obviously, I can't let Sam go without adult supervision, but I'm busy running errands, and my husband, well . . ."

She didn't have to finish the sentence. Mr. Prater's big speech at the town meeting had convinced the mayor to hold off on running Bangor out of town, but it had also made a lot of people very unhappy, specifically people Mr. Prater saw out on the water every day. As the head of the lobsterman's union, Mr. Reardon was chief among the complainants.

"I'm sorry, Stephanie," said Natalie's father. "I'd love to help, but I have to go talk to—" He caught Natalie's glare, and had the decency to look embarrassed. "I have to go to a meeting."

"Oh, okay," Mrs. Reardon said, taking Sam by the hand and quickly leading him away from the porch before the boy could figure out what was happening and begin the according meltdown. "Well, sorry to bother you."

"Not so fast," Natalie said. "I think I know an adult who can help us." She picked up Lars's leash and put on some sandals.

"Come on, Sam," she said. "We're going next door."

⟡⟡⟡⟡⟡⟡⟡⟡⟡⟡⟡⟡⟡⟡⟡⟡⟡⟡⟡⟡⟡⟡⟡⟡⟡⟡⟡⟡⟡⟡⟡⟡

Less than half an hour later, Natalie sat on the beach, watching vigilantly as Sam—now with giant water wings to accompany his giant life jacket—waddled around in the surf. Next to him, barking encouragingly, was Lars, whose leash had been left in a pile next to Natalie's beach towel in a quiet act of rebellion. And a little farther out in the water, Bangor puffed with his usual impatience, clearly not totally understanding this new addition to their usual party, but eager to figure it out as soon as possible.

Beside Natalie was Nancy Jane, who was also surveying the scene, but shifting her focus occasionally to take photos with an old camera or to jot off quick sketches of the figures splashing in the surf.

"Thank you so much for inviting me down here," Nancy Jane said, putting a colored pencil down on her towel and picking up a regular one. "I've been hoping to draw Bangor and Lars together all week."

It didn't seem all that easy. She would get halfway through a sketch of Bangor breaching the surface, and then he would dive out of sight, only to reappear again five seconds later, ten yards away. Lars didn't seem too keen on cooperating, either.

"I'm sorry," Natalie said. "It must be frustrating trying to draw something that won't stay still."

Nancy Jane shook her head, smiling warmly. "That's exactly what I want to capture," she said. "That speed. That exuberance. That joy of *life*. That's what Bangor and Lars bring to this town." She turned her smile toward Natalie. "That's what *you* brought to this town."

Although Natalie had been in a bad mood when she'd left her father at the shack, seeing the animals—and herself—through Nancy Jane's eyes made everything feel a little bit better.

Then she looked back out at the water, and her mood came crashing down again almost instantly. There, out past the far point of Perkins Cove, was a small boat with an unmistakably large cartoon face using a snorkel painted on the side. It was Diver Bob, his megaphone carrying across the water as he lectured someone about whatever poor, unsuspecting starfish he'd just pulled up from the deep. Apparently, he'd skipped out on whatever meeting Natalie's parents were having. *Good*, Natalie thought. She couldn't quite see who was on the boat from here, but there didn't seem to be many passengers. Probably just those same confused tourists who'd been at the meeting Friday night.

"Ugh," Natalie said. "Who'd want to go on one of those dumb tours? Those are for babies."

As if on cue, Sam saw the boat in the distance and started hopping up and down, yelling and waving. Lars decided to get in on the act, barking and howling happily. Bangor poked his head out of the water curiously and swiveled around.

"See?" Natalie said, laughing despite herself. "Babies!"

Rather than answer right away, Nancy Jane erased a few lines from her sketchpad and then blew on the eraser dust, allowing it to fall and mingle with the sand.

"I seem to recall," she said, "that you were one of those babies once. You used to love Diver Bob's tours."

"Yeah, well." Natalie shrugged, and then left her shoulders hunched up there around her neck. "People change."

Nancy Jane hummed softly to herself as she redid the shading on a dorsal fin, and then held it up to the light for inspection.

"And it seemed to me," she said, maintaining a casual tone, "like Diver Bob really wanted to help you and your new friends at the meeting. Your mother, too."

Natalie looked over at Nancy Jane to see if she was making fun of Natalie, but Nancy Jane's face was a mask of concentration as she finished putting the finishing touches on a drawing of a cresting wave.

For as long as Natalie had been alive, Nancy Jane had lived next door to the Praters, even acting as Natalie's babysitter on more than one occasion. When Natalie's parents went out—back when they were still together and still went out—Natalie would go over to Nancy Jane's studio. While Nancy Jane worked on painting a beautiful sunset, Natalie would sit beside her and work on a paint-by-numbers kit. Sometimes Nancy Jane would hang Natalie's paintings next to hers at the Coveside Café. Not one of them had ever sold, but it had made Natalie incredibly proud to see her work up next to a real professional's. As far as she was concerned, Nancy Jane was one of the nicest people in Ogunquit. Maybe in the whole world.

But that didn't mean Natalie agreed with her on everything.

Natalie looked back out across the ocean. Bangor did a jump for Sam, who laughed and clapped his hands, or tried to do so as much as his puffy flotation equipment would allow. From far away, she could hear the tourists on Diver Bob's boat *ooh* and *ahh*.

"Nancy Jane," Natalie said slowly, trying to work out what she wanted to ask. "Why do so many people . . . leave?"

Nancy Jane put down her sketchpad and looked directly at Natalie. "Well," she said after a long and thoughtful pause. "If this is about your mother, I'm not sure it's fair to say she *left*. She didn't go away, after all. She just went . . . somewhere else."

Natalie loved Nancy Jane, but that sentence made her roll her eyes. "That's literally what leaving is," she said.

"Is it?" Nancy Jane pointed with her pencil out at the water, where Bangor had just resurfaced close to shore.

"Take Bangor," Nancy Jane said. "One moment he's here. Then he's over there. Tomorrow he might be somewhere else entirely. But that's not the same thing as leaving someone. He's just going where the joy of life takes him."

Natalie shook her head. "No way," she said. "That's not the same thing at all. Besides, I read a lot about harbor porpoises this week, and I found out that once they find a place they like, a lot of them tend to just stay there."

When she'd read that, she'd almost danced with excitement. That meant if Bangor liked Perkins Cove—and it seemed like he did—he might stay for a long time. Maybe even forever.

"See, I think more people should be like that," Natalie went on. "When they find a good thing, they should notice it, and they should hold on to it."

"I think that's fair," Nancy Jane said. "So how come you're not doing it yourself?"

Natalie stared at Nancy Jane. That comment had made her bristle, and Nancy Jane *never* made her bristle. "What does *that* mean?" she asked.

Rather than bristle back, Nancy Jane just laughed and pointed once again at Bangor, Lars, and Sam. "This makes you happy, right?" she said. "It certainly makes *me* happy, but I feel like it makes you *very* happy."

Natalie nodded fiercely. "I love Lars," she said. "And Bangor is . . . he's a miracle. He saved Lars's life, and that's not even the most amazing part. The most amazing part is . . ." She swept her hand across the view in front of them, at the joy of three different species meeting where the water met the land. "The most amazing part is *this*."

"I thought so," Nancy Jane said. "But I'd never have guessed it from how you're sitting here worrying! Worrying is for old people, Natalie. You're young, and something amazing is happening in front of you. When I see something amazing, I try to record it." She picked up her camera and some colored pencils and waved them in front of Natalie's face. "But *you* . . . you jump right into it. You take it in your arms. And it's right there in front of you, right now. You've found your good thing, Natalie. So jump in."

Halfway through Nancy Jane's speech, Natalie had opened her mouth to protest. But as Nancy Jane had gone on, Natalie had closed her mouth again. Then she had really listened. And then she had smiled and laughed.

Nancy Jane was absolutely right.

"Thank you!" Natalie said, throwing her arms

around her neighbor in a big hug. Nancy Jane squeezed her tightly in return and then patted Natalie forcefully on the back. *Up and at 'em*, Natalie thought as she hopped up, slipped off her sandals, and ran toward the water with reckless abandon.

"Hey, Sam!" she cried giddily. "Wanna see what a harbor porpoise looks like up close?"

"Dolphin, dolphin!" Sam cried, jumping up and down in the water. Oh, well. Close enough.

Natalie picked Sam up, which was not unlike lifting a beach ball with a person in the middle of it, and waded carefully out into the water. She made sure to hold Sam well above the waves, until he was near enough to reach out and wrap his little fingers around Bangor's dorsal fin. Sam's face cracked open in a bright smile, and Natalie couldn't help but smile as well—especially when Lars paddled up to her and nudged her elbow with his nose, teasing her.

The four of them stayed there and played for the rest of the morning, until Sam got tired and asked to go home. And even though Diver Bob's boat returned halfway through, sailing right across Natalie's sight-line, she found it hard to get upset.

After all, the boat was way out there, and Natalie had her good thing right here. And she intended to hold on to it for as long as she possibly could.

CHAPTER ELEVEN

Bangor

Bangor was familiar with the concept of having too much of a good thing—after all, he had seen Uncle York eat before. But here he was, a full week into his time in Perkins Cove, and things were only getting better. Every night, he told himself this would be his last night in Ogunquit, and that when the sun rose the next morning, he would say good-bye and head back out to find his family. But when each morning rolled around, something happened to remind him how exciting this new place was: a new batch of visitors or a gift from Lars, like the morning he'd come to the beach with a little furry green ball he'd found for the two of them to push back and forth across the water. And each morning, the water got a little bit warmer, which was a very strange experience for a northern porpoise like Bangor, but certainly a new and exciting one.

And now there was this strange little human in his oddly large and brightly colored outfit, who giggled and grabbed at Bangor's fin with fingers too small and chubby to actually hurt. *The humans really never cease to produce new wonders*, Bangor marveled.

But none of the humans, even this small and very cute one, had anything on Natalie. She never yelled too loud, or played too rough, and she clearly had a lot of love for both Bangor and Lars.

But then, who wouldn't love Lars? For Bangor, Lars was maybe the best part of this all. Humans came and went—even Natalie had days where she was too busy doing human things to make it out to the beach. But Lars was there every day, as loyal as he was playful. And while he certainly enjoyed it when Bangor did tricks or flips, he didn't seem to need to be entertained. The two of them could just swim alongside each other quietly, enjoying each other's company, and that counted as playing. To Bangor, it felt deeper than a friendship; it felt like they were family. It felt like he'd found a new pod.

You already have a pod, said a voice in the back of Bangor's brain. And it was true.

But porpoises leave and find new pods all the time, Bangor thought back. And that was true, too.

But something porpoises did *not* do all the time was start new pods with strange creatures who lived on the land. It just didn't seem like good long-term planning. Right now, for example, Natalie and Lars were making their way out of the water, taking their small friend with them, and Bangor was reminded that no matter how close they grew, his new friends would go and leave him all alone every night. Every night he told himself they'd come back, and so far, every night he'd been right.

But how long could this last? What if one night they just left and never came back?

Like Bangor had done to his own family.

This was all stressful to think about. Natalie and Lars had left Bangor alone with his thoughts, and right now his thoughts weren't as fun as they usually were.

He needed to clear his head, and he *definitely* needed to eat something.

Well, he knew how to do that. He'd learned from the best. Taking one last breath for the road, Bangor disappeared underwater and turned away from the shore, swimming down and out of Perkins Cove at high speed.

As the ocean floor dropped away below him, so did Bangor's worries. The beautiful sights of the Atlantic Ocean opened up before him, distracting him completely. Jagged cliffs tumbled to dramatic depths. Colorful kelp forests swayed in the underwater waves in a dazzling array of yellows and reds and greens, punctuated by a rare blue lobster scuttling over a rocky outcrop, shining with the cobalt coloration that was only found in one out of every two million lobsters. The sunlight came down in columns from the ocean's surface, warming the water in that surprising southern way that Bangor still wasn't quite used to.

And there, suddenly showing up in Bangor's echo-location field, was the most beautiful sight of all: a massive school of herring, with no clue that Bangor was headed their way. He dove deeper to keep the element of surprise on his side, and then, when he was directly under the school, he came up for lunch.

Getting something to eat really did make him feel better. Now he felt like he had the energy to swim for hours, and that was exactly what he did. For the rest of that afternoon, Bangor explored the Gulf of Maine, eating when he pleased and surfacing whenever he wished, and never seeing the same sight twice. The ocean was so beautiful and so big.

So very, very big.

How would he ever find his family in all this water? He'd spent the week assuming he could just take a straight shot north up the coast and find them, but what if they'd gotten all turned around in the chaos of the storm and the ships? What if *he'd* gotten turned around? What if he finally did go look for them, only to find nothing at all?

Bangor didn't like that he'd lost his pod. But he would have liked it even less if he set out in search of them and wound up alone, without the pod he'd started with *or* the new one that he'd found.

It was getting dark now, and Bangor was getting nervous. Swimming through the gulf wasn't exciting anymore. It was exhausting and scary. He needed to be somewhere he felt comfortable, and he needed to rest. He needed to return to Perkins Cove, at least for a little while longer.

Bangor turned to face the direction of the coast and began to swim home for the night.

And he was over halfway there before he realized he'd thought of Perkins Cove as *home*.

CHAPTER TWELVE

Lars

Lars had never thought of anywhere as *home* in his life.

But Ogunquit was starting to get pretty darn close.

After an amazing day of playing on the beach, he and Natalie had taken Sam back to his parents' house. Nancy Jane had come along, too, to show that Sam had enjoyed good adult supervision the whole day long. At first, Lars had been a little nervous about going to the Reardons' house. Mr. Reardon clearly was not animal fan number one. After all, he'd called Lars *mangy*.

But when Mr. Reardon opened his front door and flashed the briefest of scowls, Nancy Jane just smiled sweetly, and Natalie stepped closer to Lars, and Sam cried, "Bye-bye, doggy!" as he disappeared into the house.

"Thank you!" Mrs. Reardon called from the living room.

"Thank you," Mr. Reardon echoed begrudgingly, giving Lars a nasty look. "I'm glad you didn't let my son get hurt."

"He was never in danger of being—" Natalie began, but Mr. Reardon was already closing the door. The last things they heard from inside the house were Sam yelling, "Daddy, I *love* the dolphin!" and Mrs. Reardon saying, "Honey, it's a harbor porpoise."

And then the door slammed shut.

"Well, that could have gone worse," Nancy Jane said. "Could have gone better, but could have gone worse."

But to Lars, it had all felt perfect. In that moment, he'd felt cared for, defended—loved. And as they walked back through the town, past people who stared and whispered wherever they went, even the leash around his neck didn't feel so bad, because it connected him to Natalie. And as long as he was connected to Natalie, people could whisper all they wanted, because nothing bad could happen to him at all.

Soon they passed the Coveside Café, and Nancy Jane stopped, looking in through the window thoughtfully, and then down at Lars. Lars's heart raced, thinking he might be about to get one of those delicious pastries. But instead, Nancy Jane turned her gaze to her bag full of art supplies, and then back to Lars, and then back to the window.

"Natalie," she said, "you and Lars go on home. I want to talk to Mrs. McKenzie for a bit."

"The café owner?" Natalie asked.

"That's right," Nancy Jane said, hoisting her bag a little higher on her shoulder. "I have a business proposition for her."

And with that, she disappeared through the door of the café, allowing a pastry smell to waft out that was so strong and so delicious that even Natalie seemed to catch it, although she probably wasn't going to drool about it the way Lars realized he was now doing. That was the thing about being a dog: You had amazing senses that allowed you to detect anything, but you never seemed to notice you were drooling until it was way too late.

And now Natalie noticed, looking down at Lars and laughing. "How about some food?" she asked, and Lars whimpered an affirmative. This girl just *got* him.

Natalie's father still wasn't back yet when they got to the shack, so Natalie fixed them both an early dinner. She didn't seem very happy about it, though. Upon finishing her food, she sat listlessly around the shack, occasionally glancing out at the driveway, while Lars found a nice spot on the living room carpet to rest after the morning's excitement.

After a few hours of this, Natalie appeared to come to a decision.

"I'm going to bed early, Lars. I have school tomorrow, and I . . . I don't really want to wait up for Dad right now. How about you go wait for him on the porch?"

Lars would rather have slept in Natalie's room—all the better to cheer her up—but he'd made a choice from the moment he met Natalie to do whatever she said, and this was no exception. So while she got ready for bed, Lars went out and lay down on the porch. Before long, somebody walked up the driveway, but it wasn't Natalie's father.

"Hello, Lars," Nancy Jane said, crouching down to give Lars a belly rub. Nancy Jane was the best. "I take it Jim's not back yet? I had something I wanted to speak with him about. Do you mind if I sit and wait with you?"

Rather than wait for an answer, she fished in her bag and produced a buttery croissant, holding it up for Lars to eat. As Lars practically inhaled the pastry, he wondered if there was a word for being *better* than the best.

As Nancy Jane settled down on the front-porch swing next to Lars, she pulled out her sketchpad and got to work on a drawing, while Lars got to work on licking every last molecule of croissant from his wiry whiskers. This kept both of them happily occupied until the moment he could hear Mr. Prater's footfalls turning off the main street.

"Hey, Nancy Jane," Mr. Prater grunted as he stepped onto the porch.

"Hello, Jim," Nancy Jane said, standing and quickly sliding her sketchpad into her bag. "I wanted to personally invite you to—oh, Jim, are you okay?"

Jim Prater did not look, sound, or even smell okay. The weariness rolled off him like stink off a skunk. Wherever he'd gone, he had not enjoyed himself. And, Lars realized, he also smelled slightly of—

"I'm fine," Mr. Prater said in a very not-fine voice. "I've been speaking to my—to Natalie's mother."

That was it! The woman from the town hall who smelled just like Natalie! She must have been Natalie's mom. Lars wanted to celebrate having figured out this mystery, but now didn't seem like the right time.

"Oh, you poor dear," Nancy Jane tut-tutted. "Did you two fight?"

Mr. Prater shook his head. "No, Maria is—she's fine," he said. "She seems ... happy." In a confusing development for Lars, these words seemed to make Mr. Prater even sadder.

"But the porpoise. Bangor ..." Mr. Prater trailed off. "I'm going to have to tell Natalie something soon, and she's not going to like it."

"Well, I think she's asleep, but I'll give you two some privacy, just in case," Nancy Jane said, standing up. "I have to go run some errands anyway."

She crouched down to give Lars one last rub on the belly, and then she set off across the yard and down the main road into town.

Lars didn't see a reason for the belly-rub train to stop, so he wriggled around on his back until he was upside down in front of Mr. Prater, paws in the air, ready to go. But when Mr. Prater looked down at him, Lars's hopes dropped. He knew he'd been pushing his luck, but that still didn't prepare him for just how upset Mr. Prater looked. Not just upset; he looked cross.

"You should go," Mr. Prater said. "Go on! Get!"

Wait, *what*? Lars rolled around quickly and sat up. He didn't want to panic yet, but he tilted his head as he looked up at Mr. Prater, trying to figure out what the man could possibly be thinking.

"Didn't you hear me?" Mr. Prater asked, which was a ridiculous question coming from a human, who probably couldn't hear a fly if it flew in his ear. "You need to leave!"

Okay, so it *sounded* like he meant for Lars to go. But did he really mean it? Lars hadn't come this far believing the best in people without a reason.

Sure enough, Mr. Prater sighed and sat down on his front-porch swing, shoulders slumping almost to his knees.

"I'm sorry," he said to Lars. "But it's too much. I know Natalie thinks she can take care of you and Bangor and me, but she's just one girl, and she shouldn't have to worry about all of that. She loves too much, and it's going to get her hurt."

Lars disagreed. He loved everyone, and as far as he was concerned, everyone loved him until proven otherwise. There was always enough love to go around. But something had clearly happened to Natalie's father to make him forget that, and something else had happened tonight to make it even worse.

Well, Lars would remind him. He trotted across the porch and stuck his chin in Mr. Prater's lap. That way, Mr. Prater could pet him, which would make

Mr. Prater feel better, *and* it would make Lars feel better. Being nice to people was the best.

But Mr. Prater didn't pet Lars. He just leaned back and rolled his eyes. "Look at me," he said. "I'm talking to a dog." He looked down at Lars, who put on his best puppy eyes, to no avail. "I used to talk to people," Mr. Prater continued. "Now my coworkers won't talk to me, and my wife . . . well, she talks to me, but she's not my wife. And when I tell Natalie what her mom told me tonight, Natalie won't want to talk to me, either. So I talk to a dog."

Yes, dogs provide many useful functions, Lars thought. *Which is why you should let me stay.*

"Which is why you should go," Mr. Prater said, standing up from the porch swing, gently forcing Lars to back up to the edge of the porch. "Just for a little bit. I wish it could be different."

It could be different! Lars knew it could! But if years of being a stray had taught him one thing, it was not to stick around when your welcome had worn out. So slowly, sadly, he slinked down off the porch.

"Hey, Lars," Natalie's father called out, and Lars turned around hopefully. "Be safe," Mr. Prater said.

And then he went inside and shut the door behind him.

Well, it had been nice while it lasted. Lars would just have to find Natalie sometime tomorrow after school. In the meantime, he padded down the street and tried to think: Where else in Ogunquit could he count on a warm bed or a friendly face?

Just then, a breeze blew across the main road, kicking up a smell that gave Lars the exact answer he needed: the paints and pencils and buttered pastries of Nancy Jane. She was still out running her mysterious errands, but if Lars could find her, he bet he could find a place to stay for the night.

As he followed her scent into town, he saw people walking the other way as they went home for the night, and he couldn't help but overhear snatches of their conversations as they passed. Curiously, they seemed to be talking about the very woman he was looking for.

"Nancy Jane offered me a personal invitation," someone was saying. "For Friday night."

"Me, too!" said their companion. "But she didn't tell me what I was invited *to*."

"Me, neither. She just said it was at—"

"The Coveside Café! And we're invited!" This from someone else, five minutes later, walking past the Back Porch Piano Pub. Apparently, Nancy Jane had been busy inviting a *lot* of people, but she hadn't been so clear on the specifics. Lars was excited to have a new mystery to solve, especially since it meant people weren't talking about—

"That dog," someone said from across the town square. "Over there. He weirds me out, if you ask me. Where do you think he stays at night?"

"I thought he was staying with the Praters," said someone else. "Which is fine by me. If that girl wants to take in strays, that's her business. But that porpoise—that's *all* our business. It don't belong there in the harbor."

"It's called a harbor porpoise, Steve," said the first speaker. "It's in the name."

"You know what I mean."

Lars wished he could have stayed and defended

his best friend, Bangor—or even himself—but he had a painter to find. He put his nose back down to the ground and kept following Nancy Jane's scent, which was getting stronger now. He turned off the square and entered a side street that was mostly made of tiny inns and tourist traps. Her smell was practically saturating the pavement now. He couldn't be more than a few dozen yards away from—

"Nancy Jane."

Lars's head whipped up. There, at the end of the street, was the woman he'd been looking for. And standing next to her, saying hello even as she hung a CLOSED sign on a booth labeled DIVER BOB'S BOAT TOURS, was a woman with wavy blonde hair and a strong, defined jaw.

Natalie's mother!

"Hello, Maria," said Nancy Jane.

"Hello," Natalie's mother said back. "How are you?"

"Oh, I'm doing well, thanks. I spoke to Jim just now." Nancy Jane paused as if wondering whether to add more, and then decided to do so. "And your daughter, earlier."

Natalie's mother folded her arms and bit her lip.

"How's she doing?" she asked. "Did she say anything?"

For someone who had made both Natalie and Mr. Prater so sad, she sure seemed nice—and nervous about what they thought of her.

Nancy Jane regarded her as kindly as she regarded everyone. "She misses you, Maria," said Nancy Jane. "She may have a hard time showing it, but once she's in a better place, I think she'll say so. She's getting there now, if you ask me. Her new friends have helped a lot."

Natalie's mother nodded and sighed. "That's good," she said. "But that's also a problem. The porpoise—"

"That's part of what I wanted to talk to you about," Nancy Jane said hurriedly. "On Friday, I'm holding an event that I think might do some real good for everyone in Ogunquit, human and otherwise. I wanted to invite you to—"

"Actually, there's something *I* should probably tell *you* about," Natalie's mother cut in. "Bob told me—and then I told Jim—that the porpoise really can't stay much longer."

"What?" Nancy Jane asked.

What? Lars, who had lain down to settle in for some high-quality eavesdropping, now leaped to his feet. His claws made clicking sounds on the cobblestone road, and they echoed off the walls of the inns on the otherwise silent side street. The two women peered out into the darkness, but they couldn't see Lars in the shadows.

"I'm sorry," Natalie's mother said. "Maybe we should discuss this inside. I know it's a touchy subject in the town right now. Here, follow me. Bob's just finished making chowder."

Nancy Jane followed Natalie's mother inside, taking Lars's hope of a warm place to stay with her. But Lars had bigger things to worry about now.

He'd never gone down to the beach after dark before, at least not since that first night after the storm, but now he trotted there as fast as he could, thinking of the one person he wanted to talk to, the one person who might still be out and awake at this time of night in Ogunquit. A person who wasn't, technically speaking, a person at all.

But when he got there, the beach was deserted, and he couldn't pick up a porpoise scent anywhere. What if Bangor had already left? What if he'd found out whatever Natalie's mother and all the other adults had found out, and it had made him flee? What if he'd just decided he was done with Lars, the same way Mr. Prater had, the same way everyone did in the end? What if—

And then, from far out in the cove, a whiff. A smell stronger than any of the other fish milling around in the darkened water, and coming closer. Lars perked up, ears and nose on high alert, and sure enough, there it was.

Puff!

Bangor had just been out on a fishing expedition, and now he had returned.

"Wroof!"

Lars barked once to get his friend's attention, and almost instantly, Bangor poked his head out of the water, clearly surprised to see Lars here so late.

"Eee-eee-ee-ee-e-e?" Bangor clicked. It was a greeting, but also a question: *Are you here to play? At* this *time of night?*

But Lars just whimpered, lying down on the sand, paws stretched out in front of him. He wasn't in much of a playing mood right now. He hoped Bangor would understand.

And it seemed like Bangor did understand. Rather than squeak or spin or disappear again, Bangor just stayed there, up near the surface, puffing occasionally to let Lars know he was there. And even though it was cold on the beach, Lars and Bangor fell asleep there together, lulled by the waves and the gulls, and the sound of each other's breathing.

CHAPTER THIRTEEN

Natalie

Another week had come and gone, and another Friday night had arrived only to find the entire town buzzing about one big event. It wasn't a town meeting, exactly, but practically everyone in Ogunquit had been invited, anyway, even if none of them knew what it was they'd been invited to. All anyone knew, including Natalie, was that Nancy Jane had barely been seen since Sunday, and that the Coveside Café had closed early, with a sign on the door that said COME BACK AT 7:00 P.M.! REALLY! LOVE, NANCY JANE.

If Natalie's father knew what the event was about, he hadn't told Natalie. But then again, he hadn't told Natalie much of anything this past week. When she'd woken up on Monday and discovered that Lars was nowhere to be found, her father wouldn't say if he'd seen the dog; he just stared down into his Bran Crisps and mumbled something about Lars possibly running off in the night to chase squirrels. It seemed like he knew more than he was letting on, but when Natalie found Lars outside Barnacle Barry's Seafood and Restaurant after school, begging for a doggy bag, she'd taken him right back to the shack. And even though Mr. Prater had come home that night to Lars lounging under the kitchen table while Natalie did her homework, he didn't tell Natalie whether she'd done something good or bad. He just sighed, dropped his workbag, and disappeared into his room. That had really surprised Natalie. She was used to eventually getting what she wanted from her father, but he always had the decency to at least put up a fight. To be honest, it took a lot of the fun out of it, and more worryingly, it made it seem like he was guilty of something.

Maybe it had to do with his most conspicuous silence of all: Natalie's dad still hadn't told her anything about his Sunday meeting with her mother. To be fair, Natalie had been too nervous to ask about it. She told herself she didn't want to bring it up because it was a touchy subject for him, but on some level, she knew it was because it was a touchy subject for *her*. Which made her feel embarrassed. Which made her even less likely to bring it up.

Maybe Natalie's father was just stressed because the other fishermen were giving him a hard time, but even that didn't seem quite right. Ogunquit was too small a town for anyone to *really* be mean to anyone, even the people you disagreed with, because it would always come back to bite you in the butt. A few boat owners, including Mr. Reardon, had made a big show of not taking their boats out past the drawbridge this week because they didn't want to "run into that dolphin," but that just meant more fish for everyone else, which frankly should have improved Dad's mood, not worsened it. But whenever Natalie asked him if he wanted to come down to the cove to hang out with her and Bangor—it had become an almost nightly ritual for her by now, watching her favorite harbor porpoise crisscross the cove as the setting sun lit the Atlantic Ocean on fire—her father just made up some excuse, or said he'd go next time, or left the room entirely.

And now it was the day of Nancy Jane's big secret event, and Natalie's father was still acting strange, even as they walked down to the Coveside Café, Lars trotting happily next to Natalie on his leash. Spring was always slow to come to Maine, but it had gotten a lot warmer that week, and yet another beautiful sunset was casting a soft orange light across the cobblestones and clapboard houses. The Praters had been able to leave their jackets at home, and Natalie had even put on a light summer dress. But rather than helping to cheer up Natalie's father, the balmy weather seemed to make him act shiftier than ever.

Still, it was hard for Natalie not to get excited as they got closer and closer to the café. It seemed like half the town was headed for the same destination. Sure enough, when they arrived ten minutes early, a crowd had already formed outside the locked doors. Even Mayor Maher could be spotted in the throng, standing on his tiptoes, trying to peer inside. But it was no use; someone had hung black cloth across all the windows and doors.

"Maybe Lars should stay outside for this one," Mr. Prater suggested, surveying the crowd. For once, Natalie didn't disagree. A very large number of people were about to squeeze into a very small space, and she didn't want her furry friend getting trampled underfoot. She cast a quick glance at Mayor Maher to make sure he wasn't looking, and then knelt down and removed Lars's leash.

"We'll catch up with you," she said. "It's a beautiful night outside. Go have fun."

Lars, ever the obedient dog, licked her face twice and then trotted off down the street. Natalie stood back up and looked at her father, wondering if he would say anything, but he seemed to be looking around the crowd for someone else. Weird.

Finally, seven o'clock rolled around, and Natalie could wait no longer. "Excuse me," she said, pushing her way forward. "Pardon me. Coming through." Soon she found herself in front of the crowd, and, not for the first time this month, all eyes were on her. Now she wished she had kept Lars beside her, but it was too late. She took a deep breath and knocked on the door. Almost instantly, it opened, and Nancy Jane poked her head out.

"Oh, hello, Natalie!" she said pleasantly. "I'm so glad you came. And the rest of you, as well!" She nodded at the collective citizens of Ogunquit like they were each just another neighbor dropping by for a nice chat.

There was a pause.

"Um," Natalie said.

"Would you like to come in?" Nancy Jane asked.

"*Yes!*" yelled the people of Ogunquit.

"Then, by all means," Nancy Jane said with a flourish, "be my guests!"

She threw the doors of the Coveside Café wide open, and Natalie led the townspeople into the building, like a surfer on the tip of a tidal wave.

Within seconds of entering the café, people were staring and murmuring in astonishment, Natalie included. In just two short hours, the entire place had been transformed. Tables and chairs had been hidden away somewhere; the communal bookshelf had been emptied of books; and rather than pastries and coffee machines, the café counter was loaded up with wine, cheese, and sparkling apple juice. Everything else had been cleared away, leaving room for only two things: the people in the crowd and the art on the walls.

And there was so, *so* much art on the walls.

No wonder no one had seen Nancy Jane all week. She must have been painting for *days*! And not just painting. There were sketches, charcoal drawings, giant prints of photographs, even a couple of silk-screen posters. But no matter what medium it was in, all of the art was about one thing—or, rather, two.

"It's that dang dolphin!" Mr. Reardon rumbled, looking at a beautiful painting of Bangor silhouetted at sunset.

"And the dog!" said Mr. Grundy, pointing at a sketch of Lars on the prow of the *Maria P.*

"It's actually a harbor porpoise," said someone next to Mr. Reardon.

"No," said Mr. Grundy, squinting at the sketch. "It definitely looks like a dog."

All across the room, heated discussion and debate was breaking out. Some people were amazed by the beauty of the paintings. Natalie saw a small crowd forming around a watercolor of Bangor flitting through a kelp forest. Others were less pleased. Someone pointed at a picture of Lars riding on Bangor's back and said, "That's hooey. That never happened!"

"It did, too!" Natalie said, but no one could hear her over the growing roar.

"They're beautiful," Mrs. Reardon breathed.

"They're propaganda." Mr. Reardon harrumphed.

"I want cheese!" said Sam Reardon.

"This is absolutely remarkable," Mayor Maher told Nancy Jane. "A whole themed gallery, right here in Ogunquit. You've truly outdone yourself this time, Ms. Renaud."

"Oh, please, Mayor," Nancy Jane said, looking immensely pleased with herself. "Call me Nancy Jane."

Mayor Maher turned as bright red as the sunset painting behind him, and suddenly became very interested in a silkscreen print on the other side of the room. As he excused himself, Natalie slipped in to take his place.

"This really is incredible, Nancy Jane," Natalie said. "It's some of your best work. Thank you so much for making this happen."

"I'm glad you agree!" Nancy Jane smiled mischievously at Natalie. "And I couldn't have done it without you, love. You inspired me. You and the joy that you brought this town. I just wanted to help everyone see that joy." She waved her hand across the café-turned-art-exhibition. "And because it's you, you can have any painting you want, free of charge."

"I couldn't!" Natalie gasped.

"Oh, go on," Nancy Jane said. "This only happened because of you. And it's not like anyone else is buying anything."

Looking around, Natalie realized Nancy Jane was right. Everyone was talking about the pieces, but nobody was making an effort to purchase any of them. A rubber band ball of stress began to roll around the walls of Natalie's stomach. Nancy Jane had clearly put a lot of time and energy and quite possibly money into this incredible gesture on behalf of Natalie and her animal friends. What if it all blew up in Nancy Jane's face? It was too awful to even think about.

"Oh, Nancy Jane," Natalie said. "Someone will buy something. They just have to."

Nancy Jane shrugged. "It's not about what people buy," she said. "It's about what they *feel*. If I can make them more porpoise-friendly, that'll be worth all the money in the world." But as Nancy Jane finished her drink, Natalie could see a twinge of disappointment pulling at the corners of Nancy Jane's eyes.

Gradually, the hubbub in the café was becoming a hush as they, too, realized what was expected of them, but what nobody was brave enough to do. It wasn't that nobody liked the art—the art was amazing, there was no denying it. The problem was nobody wanted to be the first to endorse the controversial dog and porpoise that the whole gallery revolved around.

And then something terrible happened—one of

those moments where, without any planning, the hush in a room became a total silence as everyone stopped talking at once.

They stared at one another.

They stared at the art.

Natalie stared at the floor, praying that something would happen.

And then a voice rang out in the silence: "How much for the charcoal porpoise?"

Everyone turned. There, standing in a suddenly very empty patch of the gallery, was a beautiful woman with wavy blonde hair and a defined jaw that she stuck out defiantly.

It was Natalie's mother.

"Three hundred dollars," Nancy Jane said. "But for you, two hundred fifty."

Natalie's mother shook her head. "I'll pay full price."

From across the room, Mayor Maher raised his hand. "And I'd like to purchase the exquisite oil painting of Perkins Cove." Everyone turned to stare at him as well, and he went bright red again. "I think it's a beautiful representation of our little town," he said defensively.

And after that, the ice was officially broken. Nancy Jane had just enough time to offer one amused wink to Natalie before she disappeared into a throng of people asking about prices and picture frames. As Natalie was pushed to the back of the fray, she saw Mrs. Reardon pulling her husband to the front and telling him, "Wouldn't that photograph of the two of them be perfect above Sam's bed?"

Natalie wanted to take a moment to celebrate Nancy Jane's success, but there was something else she had to do. She turned around and scanned the room, quickly locating the person she was looking for.

This time, it was Natalie's turn to tap her mother on the shoulder. Her mother had been calmly studying the charcoal drawing she'd just bought, but upon turning and seeing Natalie, her eyes lit up with warmth—and just a little bit of trepidation.

"Hey," Natalie said, trying to get the words out quickly before she could change her mind. "Thank you . . . for doing that. For supporting Nancy Jane. And . . . and me."

Her mother looked like she wanted to hug Natalie, but Natalie took a step back. Still, when she spoke, Natalie could hear the hug in her mother's voice.

"It was my pleasure," she said. "I miss seeing Nancy Jane every day." She smiled sadly. "And she's not the only person I miss."

"Yeah, well . . ." Natalie's first instinct was to say something mean, but she looked at the charcoal drawing of Bangor speeding through the water, and then she looked back at her mother. "How . . ." Natalie gulped, and then continued. "How is Diver Bob doing?"

Her mother's smile went from bittersweet to totally genuine. It was the first time Natalie had ever asked about her mother's new relationship.

"You can just call him Bob," she said. "And

he's . . . he's good, thank you for asking." She paused, searching for the right words. "He's more than good. He . . . makes me laugh."

Natalie gulped.

"That's good," she said. "I can see how that would be good."

Natalie's mother gazed down at her, and when she next spoke, her voice was low and earnest. "It wasn't about leaving your father behind, Natalie," she said. "He's still a very good man. It was about going where I needed to be, for me. I needed to be with someone who made me laugh. And don't be mad at your father, either. Sometimes, letting go of someone isn't giving up. It's helping."

This was officially too much for Natalie. "Well, anyway," Natalie said, starting to back away. "Just thought I'd say hi. And thanks. For buying the drawing."

"Of course," her mother said. "It's beautiful. It'll be good to have something to remember Bangor by."

"What?" Natalie froze, her foot in the middle of a backward step. "What does that mean?"

Natalie's mother blinked in confusion, and her

mouth opened in a round O. "Did—did your father not tell you?" she asked. "I thought—"

"Tell me *what*?" Natalie's voice came out all scratchy; her throat had suddenly gone very dry.

Natalie's mother looked both ways, and then closed the distance between her and her daughter, speaking in a quiet voice. "Bob did some research on harbor porpoises, Natalie. They have to live in water that's below sixty degrees. And the water's getting warmer down here really quickly—too quickly. Bangor will have to go north soon, for his own good. He needs to be in his own habitat."

Natalie felt like the room was spinning. In all the reading and research she had done on harbor porpoises, she hadn't come across this information. How had she missed this?

"I told your father," her mother said. "I really thought he'd told you, Natalie. I'm sorry."

Natalie turned and looked wildly around the gallery until she saw her dad, halfway to popping a cube of cheese in his mouth. When he saw the expression on his daughter's face, he froze mid-cheese-pop.

For the second time in an hour, Natalie pushed her way through a crowd, but this time she didn't bother with "Excuse me." This time, she yelled.

"How *could* you?!"

"Natalie, I—" Her dad didn't even bother to ask what was happening; he clearly knew. "You seemed so happy, and I didn't want to ruin it—"

"Well, that worked out *great!*"

Once again, everyone was staring at Natalie, but this time she really didn't care. She wanted everyone to see her father for the jerk that he was. But she realized now that she didn't actually want to see him herself, or look at him at all. She just wanted to get out of there.

So she ran.

Outside, the last minutes of sunset made the town more beautiful than ever, but she couldn't enjoy it. Tears stung her cheeks as she ran down Main Street, heading for the only place life still made sense, the only place where she knew she had friends she could count on.

Sure enough, when she got to Perkins Cove, there

they were—Bangor, squeaking in the surf, and Lars, who must have made a beeline for the beach the moment Natalie had sent him off. The two friends were taking advantage of every last moment of sunlight to swim through the water, but when Bangor saw Natalie, he barked a hello. She wiped the tears from her eyes as she made her way to them, kicking off her sandals but neglecting to do anything else to her clothes. Right now, she didn't even care if her dress got wet. She just waded right on into the water. It was the warmest it had been all year.

Her mother was right.

Lars swam up to say hello, and his nuzzling nose was as comforting as usual. But as Bangor came to join them, Natalie looked directly into one of his deep, black eyes, and she knew something to be true: If Bangor was ever going to be happy—if he was going to stay alive—he would have to go north, and break up this friendship for good.

And if he wouldn't do it, then she would have to do it for him.

With one hand, Natalie reached out and pulled Lars close. With the other, she put a calming hand on Bangor's side as she leaned in and gently, lightly, kissed him on the melon.

And then she began to think of a plan.

CHAPTER FOURTEEN

Lars

This town meeting was even louder than the last, but there were a few things about it that made Lars excited to be there.

For one thing, he'd snuck into the courthouse while people were setting up, found the dreaded gavel, picked it up like it was a bone, and hidden it behind a tree outside the town hall where no one would be tempted to use it.

For another thing, someone had hung a picture of him in the hall. He'd seen it on his way back in. He thought it was a very good picture of him, and he thought more public buildings should consider hanging up pictures of him, in general.

But the most exciting thing of all was that Natalie

was standing behind the judge's lectern looking out at the people of Ogunquit.

Because Natalie had called this meeting herself.

The night before, when Natalie had found him and Bangor at the beach, she'd only stayed in the water for a little while, staring strangely at Lars and Bangor before apparently coming to some sort of decision. Then she'd led Lars back to shore, put the leash on his neck, and ran with him to the Coveside Café, her dress still dripping wet. Mayor Maher was just leaving as they arrived, carrying a large canvas under his arm, and he stopped when he saw Natalie.

"Miss Prater," he said. "I think I owe you an apology. It's been a week now, and rather than cause any problems, your porpoise friend seems to have brought us all together. And, of course, your dog, too." He gave an obliging but curt nod down to Lars, who wagged his tail a few times for etiquette's sake.

"About that," Natalie said. "Will the courthouse be in use tomorrow morning? I think we need to call an emergency town meeting."

The mayor frowned. "No, it should be unoccupied," he said. "But why do you want to—"

"Great, thanks. Bye!" Natalie was already heading into the café, and Lars, bound by leash and loyalty, followed hot on her heels. Once inside, Natalie went from person to person, spreading the news: "Emergency town meeting! Tomorrow morning! Ten a.m. at the courthouse! Be there!"

You had to hand it to the townspeople: Most would shy away from the prospect of two mysterious townwide gatherings in twenty-four hours, but not the people of Ogunquit. Here they all were now, on a Saturday morning, packed right back into the courthouse, eager to see what crazy twist this tale would take next.

Lars was pretty eager himself. He sat dutifully at Natalie's right-hand side, ready to lend any moral support she might need while she addressed the town. To Lars's right-hand side was Natalie's mother, holding hands with the infamous Diver Bob. On the other side of the lectern, to Natalie's left, was Mr. Prater, dressed up in a shabby suit that, as far as Lars's nose was concerned, could have used a good dry cleaning. And finally, on the far left, looking thoroughly perplexed by how any of this had come to pass, was Mayor Maher.

"Alright, everyone," Natalie said, trying to get the room to quiet down. Mayor Maher had lent her a microphone, but her voice was still getting lost in the crowd. "Can we—where'd that gavel go?—can everyone please be—"

Lars barked as loud as he could, and the whole room fell into a stunned silence.

"Thank you, Lars," Natalie said. "And thank you, everyone, for coming on such short notice. It has recently been brought to my attention that we have a problem on our hands—one that has to do with, of course, Bangor."

"With *what*?" called out Barry Rosenberg, owner of Barnacle Barry's Seafood and Restaurant.

"The porpoise," Natalie explained.

"So you agree he presents a problem!" Mr. Reardon cried triumphantly. Lars let out a low growl, but Natalie scratched absentmindedly behind his ears, and he fell quiet. This was her time to speak.

"With all due respect, Mr. Reardon," Natalie said, "the problem isn't Bangor himself." She took a deep breath and turned to her mother, who nodded encouragingly. Natalie turned back to the mic. "The problem is the environment he's in. He needs to be in a different one."

As Natalie explained what her mother and Diver Bob had figured out together, Lars felt his heart sink, even as he was amazed by Natalie's courage. Bangor was going to have to leave? For how long? Could he come back?

As if reading Lars's mind, Natalie turned to the right. "Tell them what you told me last night after the gallery, Dive—" She paused. "I mean . . . Bob."

At that, Lars could smell the surprise on both of Natalie's parents. Diver Bob, for his part, seemed as implacably cheerful as ever as he shuffled on up to the lectern.

"Thank you, Natalie," he said brightly, before turning to address the room. "It's true that harbor porpoises ought to live in waters well below sixty degrees, and once we hit tourist season, Ogunquit's water temperatures will exceed that on a regular basis. In water that warm, Bangor risks overheating, or getting sick, or possibly something . . . much worse."

The courtroom erupted in surprised whispers, but died down so Diver Bob could continue.

"When I heard that this porpoise had a tag on him from the Bangor Sea Lab, I reached out to some of my marine biologist friends there, and they confirmed that the porpoise we call Bangor is one they've been tracking since he was just a calf—a member of a normally sedentary pod historically located about a hundred miles north of Ogunquit, where the water stays below sixty degrees year-round. We don't know how they got separated, or where the pod is now, but we do know one thing: Once a harbor porpoise finds a place it likes to live, it often tends to stay there. So while we know where Bangor came from, we can't be sure that he knows, or that he'll know enough to make an effort to return there—to his family."

"What does this have to do with any of us?!" called out Mr. Grundy.

"For the answer to that question," Diver Bob said, "I'd like to turn the floor over to Jim Prater."

There was a murmuring in the crowd. Everyone in town knew about the tension between Bob Dugnutt and Jim Prater.

But Mr. Prater was acting like a new man today. Lars had noticed the tension between Natalie and her father all week, ever since he'd tried to push Lars away on Sunday, and then oddly acted like it had never happened for the rest of the week. He'd seemed, more than anything, like a man running on guilt and nerves. But now, dressed up in what was quite possibly his nicest suit, Lars got the sense that Mr. Prater was doing his best to right anything he'd made wrong by doing his best for his daughter—even if it meant working together with the man he didn't get along with.

"Thank you, Bob," he said, stepping up to speak. And Natalie, who just last night had barely been able to look at her father, now squeezed his hand softly: *Thank you, Dad.*

"Hey, guys," Mr. Prater said, waving awkwardly at the assembled gang of fellow fishermen. "It's been a crazy couple of weeks—for my daughter, for me, and for all of us here in Ogunquit. But before things go back to normal, one last crazy thing is going to happen. It's an idea Natalie came up with last night, and I'm very proud of it. But I'm here to personally speak to you upstanding citizens"—he scanned his eyes across the face of each and every fisherman in the audience—"because for this crazy thing to happen, we're going to need some help—and we're going to need it from every last one of you."

The entire front right of the room broke out in protestations, questions, and scoffs. Mr. Prater stood back and waited for everyone to calm down, but even when they did, one person still had his hand up: Mr. Reardon, who was looking directly at Natalie.

"Yes?" Natalie asked, calling on the man who was almost forty years her senior.

"Why the change of heart?" Mr. Reardon asked skeptically. "Just last week, you were so eager to keep this dolphin"—he paused, looking around sheepishly to see if his wife was nearby—"this *harbor porpoise* around, health or safety be darned. Now you're practically leading the committee to drive it out of Dodge. Why should we believe you want our help making it leave?"

Lars craned his neck up at Natalie, eager to hear the answer. He obviously trusted his human completely, but if she was going to send Bangor away from Ogunquit, he hoped she had a really, *really* good reason.

Natalie looked first to the left, at her father, and then to the right, at her mother. Lars had never seen them all stand together like this. He wondered how long it had been since they'd been able to. And when Natalie turned back to the mic, she was almost smiling—almost. She may as well have been. A genuine smile was one of those things Lars could just smell.

"It's not about the porpoise leaving," she explained. "It's about helping it to go where it needs to be." She looked at her mother. "Sometimes, letting go of something isn't giving up—it's helping."

Lars wasn't sure where those words had come from, but the moment Natalie said them, both her and her mother's scents turned into a rose-gold wash of love and pride. Sitting there between them, taking it in, Lars felt like the luckiest dog in the world.

Mr. Reardon grunted. "Well, alright, then," he said. "I'm sorry to have interrupted. Please, tell us this plan of yours."

"Alright," Natalie said, leaning forward.

And she told them.

CHAPTER FIFTEEN

Natalie

That night was even warmer than last night. Twenty-four hours ago, that would have terrified Natalie, serving as a reminder of the sad secret her mother had told her.

But after she'd had time to come to terms with it, she saw it another way: A warm, beautiful night like tonight was the perfect opportunity to go down to the beach and spend one last playtime with her favorite porpoise.

She'd put on her best swimsuit. She'd found the Frisbee that had been tucked away in the Praters' shed since last November and threw it for Lars a few times, in case he wasn't familiar with the concept. If he wasn't, he caught on quick. And then she'd put it in a beach bag with some other items and walked with Lars and her father down to Perkins Cove.

Since their big blowup Friday night, Natalie's father had been doing everything he could to make it up to his daughter. He'd been the first to encourage her crazy plan, and he'd been the one to reach out to Diver—to *Bob*—and Natalie's mother, and bring them all together to hammer out the details. But truth be told, Natalie had been ready to forgive him before she'd even made it back from the beach. She'd spent a lot of time angry at her parents this year. Too much time. Right now, she had bigger things to worry about.

And bigger things to celebrate.

When they got to the beach, Bangor was just swimming back in from another one of his food runs out in the gulf. The setting sun threw its rays across the waves like rose-colored oil sliding over the water. It looked like a scene from one of Nancy Jane's paintings. Actually, it looked like the paint itself.

Thinking of Nancy Jane made Natalie smile, just

as much as Lars running to greet Bangor with all his characteristic enthusiasm made her smile.

"You've found your good thing," Nancy Jane had said. "Jump in."

She turned to her father as she pulled the Frisbee from her bag. "Want to come in with me?"

"Oh, I don't know," he said, but his eyes were already out on the water, where Bangor had just done a barrel roll. "I'm wearing my work shorts, and—"

"I'll race you," Natalie said, and she was off, and behind her she heard the sound of her father's wallet, cell phone, and keys hitting the sand as he emptied his pockets and ran after her.

That evening was the best good thing she'd ever had. The Frisbee turned out to be a hit with dog and porpoise alike, and after some convincing that large humans could be just as okay to play with as small humans, Bangor and Mr. Prater managed to unite for a quality splash contest. Natalie knew she might never get the chance to do something like this again, and rather than let it make her sad, she used it to make every second count, wringing as much fun out of the moment as possible.

Well, maybe it still made her a little sad. But maybe that was okay. Maybe that was life.

Soon the sun had set completely, and the stars began to emerge over the Atlantic Ocean.

"Okay," Mr. Prater said, attempting to rub some of the salt water out of his eyes with his equally salt water–covered knuckles. "We should get home soon."

Natalie nodded. The plan was set to begin early the next morning, and they'd need all the rest they could get beforehand.

"Do you want to say good-bye to Bangor?" Mr. Prater asked. At the sound of his name, Bangor, ever the attention hog, released a hopeful *puff*.

Natalie considered the porpoise warmly, and then shook her head. "No," she said. "I'll do it tomorrow."

Or never, she thought. The truth was, she didn't know if she'd have the guts to say good-bye.

Her father shrugged. "Suit yourself," he said. "C'mon, Lars! Let's go home!"

The three of them turned to make their way out of the water and froze. Someone was standing on the beach by all of their belongings, watching so quietly in the darkness that Natalie hadn't even noticed they were there.

It was Natalie's mother.

"Hello, Jim," she said as her ex-husband and daughter approached her. "Hello, Natalie. And hello, Lars." She crouched down and opened her arms for a hug at dog height, and after a moment's consideration, Lars seemed to decide this was acceptable, and trotted happily into the hug.

As Maria Prater scratched Lars's back, she looked up at Mr. Prater and Natalie.

"I realized I'd never actually seen it," she said. "The two of them—or the three of you—or, I guess, the *four* of you—all playing together." She gave Lars one last pat and stood up. "It was wonderful," she said. "I'm glad I got to see it."

Natalie's father seemed unsure of what to say, but Natalie was getting better at this, and she stepped in for him.

"I'm glad you got to see it, too," Natalie said, and the best part was, she meant it.

Even in the darkness, Natalie's mother's smile was radiant. "Thank you," she said.

Then she put her hands on her hips and bit her bottom lip.

"There's something else I came to tell you, though," she said. "Bob received word from the people at Bangor Sea Lab. They got in touch with some of their colleagues at a different lab in Belfast who've also been tracking a member of the pod. They confirmed the pod's current location. They're a little bit farther south than normal, but they're all together, and all in about the area we'd anticipated."

"That's fantastic!" Mr. Prater said. "Then we can lead Bangor right back to his family!" He turned to Natalie. "Isn't that great?"

Natalie wasn't sure what to say. It was all becoming real now. In less than twelve hours, this whole adventure would hopefully be coming to a happy ending. But the only way for her to reach that happy ending was to get through the sad ending.

Below her, Lars, clearly deciding he wasn't getting any more pats from Natalie's mother, wandered back to Natalie and laid his head down on her feet. His whiskers tickled at her sandy ankles. Where once his fur had been wiry and scraggly, Lars's coat was now shinier and healthier, even after just a couple of weeks with the Praters. Nothing had been better for him than being with a family that loved him, in an environment where he could be safe.

It's not giving up, Natalie thought. *It's helping.*

"Great," she said. "That's great news." She leaned down, picked up her beach bag, and hoisted it over her shoulder. "Now, let's go get some sleep."

Because tomorrow morning, she thought, *we save a porpoise.*

CHAPTER SIXTEEN

Bangor

Because Bangor never really slept, Bangor never really "woke up," at least in the traditional sense. And because of that, Bangor had never really experienced a rude awakening.

But Sunday morning, floating in the middle of Perkins Cove, he just about got one.

The morning started like any other since Bangor had come to Ogunquit. As he bobbed up and down in the gentle waves of dawn, Bangor faced the shore, resting the left side of his brain and using his right side to enjoy the feeling of the sun sliding slowly across his back.

He'd been noticing it more and more recently— when the sun shone down here in the south, it really *shone.* They had sunshine where he was from in the north, of course, but it never seemed to work quite as hard or make things quite as warm as the sun that fell on Ogunquit. Every morning, the water around Bangor got just a little bit warmer, just a little bit faster. He'd never felt anything like it.

I'm not sure you're supposed *to feel anything like it,* said a voice in the back of Bangor's head. Bangor tried to push the thought away, but there was something about the tone of concern that reminded Bangor of someone.

He realized it reminded him of Kittery—of his mother.

Now there was a thought Bangor *really* didn't want to deal with this early in the morning. *I'll worry about my pod later,* he thought. *Right now, I need to get some rest.*

But the side of him that was awake registered a new noise, one that started soft and then gradually got louder. It was the drawbridge, slowly creaking into its open position. The bridge, with its chorus of squeaks and groans, signaled the start of the workday in Ogunquit. Bangor was used to this by now, and he was also used to what came next: the thrum of boat engines starting up as a handful of fishermen began their daily trip out of the harbor.

But this morning, it quickly became clear that something unusual was happening. Rather than stopping at three or four engines, the boats kept roaring to life, one after another—and then another and another and another—until it was impossible for Bangor to even halfway sleep through the din. His left eye snapped open in irritation, and he turned toward the open drawbridge to squeak his disapproval at the boats that slipped one by one out of the harbor.

"E-e-e-e-e-e!"

It was no use, of course. There was no way the humans would hear him over their noisy vessels, which were only getting noisier still, as more and more of them started up their engines.

And yet, for a brief moment, Bangor thought that he might have heard someone call back over the engines. The unexpected noise came from far across the water, where the first of the boats was just now clearing the edge of Perkins Cove. The noise sounded like . . . barking? Instinctively, Bangor lurched through the water toward the mystery sound, which so resembled the voice of his good friend Lars. But if it actually was Lars, Bangor was unable to tell for sure, because within seconds, even more engines had turned on in the harbor, and it soon became impossible to hear anything else.

Bangor came to a halt, confused to the point of being unable to move. In all of his time here, he'd never known the fishermen to do anything remotely like this. It felt like every water molecule in the cove was vibrating with the sound of the whole fishing fleet come to life. It made echolocation impossible, it hurt Bangor's head, and it caused his initial sense of irritation to quickly give way to panic.

Clearly, it was time to get out of the harbor. But where could he go? By now, there were half a dozen boats already out on the open water, and rather than dispersing, they'd all perched just past the edge of Perkins Cove, as if idling in wait just for Bangor.

Maybe they *were* waiting for him. Maybe that was what the barking had been: a signal from Lars to come find him, to follow the boats out into the Atlantic. But why?

Well, Bangor wouldn't find out by sitting around here. With one last irritated chirp—*Fine, I'm coming*—he took off through the water, toward the open water and away from the wall of sound blasting behind him.

But the moment he started to move, the wall of sound began to follow him—and fast.

Bangor couldn't be sure of how many boats were peeling out of the harbor and into the wider waters of Perkins Cove. In that moment, he couldn't be sure of anything. The boats, already so terribly noisy when they were just idling in the harbor, became even worse when they were racing toward him, bombarding Bangor with an overwhelming racket. Within seconds, all of the poor porpoise's remaining senses were obliterated.

It was awful. Waves of sound and waves of water crashed and combined and broke apart around him. Any clicks he sent out in front of him seemed to come back from beside and behind him. Bangor darted this way and that, trying to find a direction that would take him out of the cove and away from the chaos, but the world had become directionless. Up was down. Down was up.

From somewhere in the back of Bangor's brain, pushing its way through the pandemonium, came a thought that made him feel, somehow, even worse: This was what Uncle York must have experienced when that first fleet had fallen upon them. At the time, Uncle York had suddenly become unable to swim straight to save his life, and now, as Bangor ducked and rolled through thrashing water, he felt the same way. It was just as terrible to go through as it had been to witness—and it was even worse for Bangor knowing that he had abandoned his uncle, and possibly the rest of his pod, to suffer this terrifying feeling alone. What if Bangor never made it out of here, and the last time his family saw him was while they swam through something like this?

Bangor couldn't stand that thought. He had to make his escape, and he had to do it soon.

But as the boats bore down on top of him, Bangor didn't know if he would ever get the chance.

CHAPTER SEVENTEEN

Natalie

For Natalie, the morning started with a parade.

Or it almost did. Technically, the morning started with Lars leaping onto Natalie's bed and taking one big lick from the bottom of her chin to the inside of her nose. His methods were sloppy, but his timing couldn't have been any better—it was quarter past five in the morning, five minutes before Natalie's alarm was set to go off and twenty minutes before the sun was supposed to rise, at least according to the *Fisherman's Almanac* that Natalie had pored over in the Praters' kitchen the night before. And if they'd done as she'd asked, soon every fisherman and lobsterman in Ogunquit would be waking up as well, rolling out of bed for the big day.

As Natalie went to the bathroom to wash the dog slobber off her face, she hoped desperately that those alarms actually were going off across town. She figured she had only one chance to pull this plan off, and she didn't want to think about what might happen if today didn't go right. By the time she was dressed and at the kitchen table, she was too nervous to even speak, and together with her father—who never spoke much in the early mornings, anyway—she wolfed down a quick and quiet breakfast while Lars not-so-quietly wolfed down a bowl of fish. Then they looked at each other, nodded, gathered up their stuff, and made their way to the front door and out into the dawn.

"Do you think anyone's actually going to come and help?" Natalie asked, bending down to fasten the leash around Lars's neck. "I mean, at least a few people will, right?"

Her father, who had just finished locking the door to the shack, turned to face the street.

"I think we'll be fine," he said with a smile, pointing out toward the street. Natalie stood back up and followed his gaze—and gasped.

Because that's when she saw the parade.

To be fair, it wasn't totally unusual for the boat owners of Ogunquit to get up before sunrise, especially the ones who had to work. But for every single one of them to head for the cove at the same time, and on a Sunday no less, was an extraordinary thing to think about—and, it turned out, even more extraordinary to behold. Now, in the early almost-light, tramping down a road that was normally just stirring to life at this time of the morning, was an ever-growing stream of seafaring townspeople, pouring forth from their porches and garage doors, all of them headed in the same direction that any stream inevitably ran toward—the sea.

And they weren't the only ones. As an awestruck Natalie led Lars and her father down the driveway to take their places in the procession, she saw still more people she recognized from around town. The spouses of the fishermen had come along to see what all the fuss was about, and that meant their children had come, too, running between the legs of the adults or bouncing up and down in their parents' arms if they hadn't quite woken up yet. As the sun broke over Ogunquit, Natalie's heart filled with joy and gratitude.

"I don't believe it," she breathed.

"I do." Her father smiled. "You're always going out of your way to help others. Now we all get to help you."

Hearing it put like that almost made Natalie tear up, but it reminded her of something else. She had work to do, and she wasn't going to get a better chance than now to do it. As more and more people joined the parade, Natalie and Lars ran back and forth from fisherman to fisherman, reminding everyone exactly what they had to do: who would be on the first wave of boats out of the harbor; who would hang back and bring up the rear; what channel to set their radios to; what signal to listen for; and most importantly, how crucial it was that they not do anything at all until they got that signal.

In short, Natalie did everything in her power to make sure that absolutely everything went according to plan.

Just half an hour later, everyone was right where

they were supposed to be: The boats now surrounded Bangor in the harbor.

But things were not going according to plan.

"What's taking him so long?" Mr. Prater asked. The *Maria P.* bobbed up and down at the very edge of Perkins Cove, along with the half dozen other boats that made up the first wave. They were all waiting expectantly for something to happen—even as something continued to very much not happen.

"I don't know! He seemed to be getting it a few minutes ago." Natalie leaned over the gunwale and peered through a pair of binoculars.

The starting of the engines seemed to have stirred Bangor awake, just as Natalie had hoped. She'd seen his fin turn this way and that, as if trying to locate the source of the sound. And it was possible she'd imagined it, but she could have sworn that he'd turned to face the *Maria P.* at one point—the point when Lars, overcome with excitement, had leaped up, planted his two front paws on the gunwale, and begun barking at the top of his lungs. But the farther out they got, the less Bangor seemed able to keep his bearings focused on the *Maria P.*

None of this kept Lars from barking like his life depended on it. Just a few weeks ago, Natalie reflected, this would have felt like getting everything she wanted—Lars riding with them in the boat with her father's blessing. But life was more complicated now, and Natalie had a problem to solve before she could truly enjoy anything.

"We can't just wait around forever." That was Mr. Grundy's voice, crackling over the radio.

"Nobody does anything until you hear the word *go*," Mr. Prater barked, but he was looking back and forth between Natalie and the bay with an expression of increasing concern.

"Be patient with the porpoise," said Diver Bob. "All this commotion is probably very confusing for him." Even though he wasn't *technically* a fisherman, Diver Bob still had a boat, and still volunteered to help out. That was another thing that was probably pretty nice, but Natalie didn't have time to focus on that right now.

"Come on, Bangor..." Natalie muttered under her breath. And even though she knew it couldn't possibly make a difference, she let out a low, slow, hopeful whistle, like the kind she'd heard Bangor make so many times since meeting him.

And at that moment, Bangor finally turned back toward the open water and began to swim straight for the Praters' boat.

"Yes!" Natalie exclaimed.

"There we go!" Diver Bob whooped.

"Did he say *go*?" asked someone over Mr. Prater's radio.

"Wait!" cried the Praters.

But it was too late. One of the boats in the harbor roared to life, and a split second later, the rest of them followed suit. Even from all the way out at the edge of the cove, the sound was tremendous.

"It's too soon!" Natalie cried. And, indeed, as she watched in dismay, the gray streak under the water that was Bangor suddenly took a hard left from his original path, and then a right, and then a dozen crazy dives in no clear direction. The sound of the fleet seemed to have disoriented him, and it looked like he was in a state of complete confusion, or possibly even in pain.

"Stop!" Natalie cried. "Dad, tell them to stop!"

But the *Sammy Boy*, Mr. Reardon's boat, was already trundling out from under the drawbridge—and Bangor was already tearing toward the open water frantically, taking a blind stab at escape.

"He's making it out!" someone pointed out over the radio. "That's good, right?"

"That's even worse!" Natalie said, clearing the deck in two strides and snatching the radio from her father's hand. "What if he goes out there all confused and we lose him?"

We're not going to get a second chance at this! she wanted to yell, but Mr. Grundy, who was just two boats over from them on the *Kelly Natasha*, was already cutting in. "He's going to pass our boat any moment!"

"Stop all the boats!" Natalie said, thrusting the radio back at her father. "Tell them all to stop!"

"Cut your engines! Cut your engines!" Mr. Prater looked out at the drawbridge, where a dozen boats were now well out into the cove. When he turned back to his daughter, his eyes were wide. "I don't think they're all listening, Natalie."

Well, Natalie thought, *if they aren't going to respond to any of the signals they agreed to, I'll just have to come up with a new one.*

"Hold on to Lars," Natalie said, picking up the leash she'd dropped to the deck. She placed it in her father's hand before making her way rapidly to the edge of the boat.

"What's your plan—*Natalie Prater, you stop this instant!* Everybody, cut your engines!"

But Natalie didn't have time to stop, and she had no idea if anyone did cut their engines just then, because she was too busy jumping off the boat.

Splash! Just like Lars had done all those nights ago, Natalie plunged into the ocean, and for a split second, the sound of her father roaring into his radio was muffled by water and the rush of air bubbles. Then her life jacket yanked her back up, even as momentum carried the rest of her body down, and Natalie breached the surface, feeling like gravity had just tried to tear her body in two. As salt water stung her nostrils and eyes, she gasped and coughed and tried to get a sense of her surroundings.

The first thing she noticed was the unexpected quiet of the cove, as all the boats surrounding her suddenly stopped. The fishermen gazed down at Natalie from their boats, amazed by the crazy girl who had jumped into the water.

The second thing Natalie noticed was Lars, barking bloody murder just a few yards behind her.

And the third thing she noticed was Bangor, missing Natalie by mere inches as he shot straight past her and made his way out into the open water.

There wasn't time for Natalie to think; she could only try to get Bangor's attention using the first method that sprang to mind. She put two fingers in her mouth and whistled as loud as she possibly could. The whistle went on for as long as her wave-battered lungs could manage, and when it was done, an eerie silence fell over the cove. All the boats were stationary. Lars, perhaps impressed by Natalie's approximation of a dog whistle, had ceased his barking for at least the current moment. And from out past the *Maria P.*, though Natalie strained her ears to hear, there was nothing at all—no sign that any of this had worked.

And then:

Puff!

The sound wasn't far away. Natalie's head was well above water, but she still gasped and held her breath.

Puff!

And that one was closer still.

Natalie exhaled. Bangor was coming back!

A cheer went up among the men before Mr. Prater hissed into his radio: "Don't scare him, guys, be quiet!" But it was like Bangor had fixed on to a homing beacon, and that beacon was Natalie. Soon she could make out his silver shape pushing past the bottom of the *Maria P.*, and then circling her in wide arcs that drew ever tighter, until finally, miraculously, he was right in front of her.

Bangor poked his head out of the water and eyed her warily. Natalie almost laughed with delight, but she was as nervous about spooking Bangor as her father was. Slowly and carefully, she reached out her hands, palms up, before turning them over to rest on Bangor's melon.

"Hey," she said softly.

"*Sree-e-e-e-e-e!*" Bangor released a shrill whistle. Over his dorsal fin, Natalie saw Lars's ears perk up, and he pulled at his leash, though Mr. Prater held on tight.

"I'm sorry we scared you," Natalie said, still speaking in gentle and measured tones, barely louder than the waves lapping around her. "It wasn't supposed to be like this. We thought you would follow us out first, and then everyone else could bring up the rear. So you would get that we were all going somewhere— so that you'd feel like we were going together."

She tried to nod her head out toward the open water. Bangor puffed again, and then ducked below the surface of the waves. Natalie fell forward a little, losing the balance she'd had on Bangor's head, though her life jacket righted her swiftly. When Bangor emerged again, he was a few feet farther away. He whistled again, even shriller this time.

"Hey," Natalie heard her father say from the boat. "Cut it out, Lars."

Natalie kept her eyes on Bangor.

"You don't understand, do you?" she said sadly.

"I get it. You're scared out of your mind, and you're an animal, and one who doesn't like change, to boot. I know how that feels. I just wish there was some way I could make you feel better."

But she didn't know what that could possibly be. She felt like she'd tried everything.

Meanwhile, the fussing from the boat was getting louder.

"I'm serious," Mr. Prater said. "Stop yanking, you're giving my hand rope burn—hey—ow—*hey!*"

And then there was a single bark and a yelp and a skittering of paws and claws against the surface of the deck, and then a *splash*. And as Natalie and Bangor both turned around to see what was going on, Natalie felt her heart rise at an unexpected thought: Maybe, she realized, they hadn't tried everything . . .

CHAPTER EIGHTEEN

Lars

For the record, Lars had thought this was a pretty silly plan from the get-go.

To be fair, there were some parts of it he didn't understand. Even after he'd heard Diver Bob and everyone else explain it at the big town meeting, he'd still been unclear as to why exactly they had to make Bangor leave town. He got that it had something to do with the summer temperature, but Lars wasn't crazy about heat, either. And did he go north every time the summer rolled around? No, he just shed his winter fur, like a normal animal. Couldn't Bangor do that? Apparently not. Maybe it was a porpoise thing.

But then there were parts of the plan that he felt like he *did* understand, that the humans did not. Like all the noise. Lars could have told anyone, had they bothered to ask him, that starting up an entire town's worth of boats without warning was going to be way more scary than reassuring for Bangor. Humans just didn't get what it was like to have ears that actually worked—that really *heard* things, rather than only the loudest of sounds. That's why he'd spent so much time barking as the *Maria P.* made its way out of the cove that morning: He wanted Bangor to hear a friendly sound, rather than the incoming onslaught of Ogunquit's engines.

I'm here! he'd tried to let Bangor know. *It's okay! Come with us!*

But clearly, it hadn't worked. The porpoise couldn't understand the dog, the humans couldn't understand the porpoise—and Lars felt like he could understand everyone, but he couldn't make anyone *listen.* Even now, watching Natalie and Bangor meet in the water, Lars whimpered in sympathy every time Bangor released one of his high-pitched whistles. He strained at his collar, but Mr. Prater just pulled tighter on his leash. Lars didn't blame him for being tense; the man was clearly uncomfortable already having one of his passengers out in the water, let alone two. But Lars couldn't help it. He wanted to swim right out there and tell Bangor everything was going to be alright.

Natalie was trying to do the same thing, but whatever she was saying to Bangor just wasn't getting through. It hurt for Lars to watch two people he loved fail to understand each other, just as it had hurt to watch Natalie not realize how much her mother still loved her, the same way it had hurt when Mr. Prater kicked Lars off the porch.

Lars understood why all those mistakes had happened: Humans thought they could solve all their problems by thinking about them and talking about them. But as a dog, Lars knew it didn't work like that. The best way to make people feel better was to show them they were cared for in a way they couldn't miss. Even when people were confused or upset, some actions could be understood in any language: a hug from a mother, or a big old lick on the face from a friend. Or the unexpected, lifesaving appearance of a porpoise's back under your paws just when you needed it most.

And in that moment, Lars finally understood what he had to do.

Sorry about this, Mr. Prater, Lars thought, yanking on his leash. The leash slid forward through Mr. Prater's hands. Mr. Prater cried out with surprise, but he didn't let go, so Lars pulled harder—and harder— until finally Mr. Prater released the leash and Lars dashed madly across the deck. Behind him, he heard Mr. Prater try to grab at the leash, but Lars was already catapulting himself up off the deck and onto one of the coolers, and then off the boat, through the air, and into the water.

Splash! As the world went dark around him, Lars remembered how it had felt the first time he went over the edge of the *Maria P.*, when he had slid straight into the ocean and all had seemed lost. It was a scary memory to think about, especially as he paddled his way furiously up toward the surface. But what was happening now didn't seem half as scary to Lars. After all, this wasn't some accidental fall. Now Lars was a dog with a mission.

The moment he got back above water, Lars spun this way and that before finding what he was looking for: Natalie, staring at him in shock, and Bangor, a few feet away, watching Lars closely. Lars let out his customary short bark of greeting—*Hello!*—and then quickly made his way toward the porpoise.

Over the past couple of weeks, Lars had become extremely good at doggy paddling, but Bangor still helped him out by closing some of the distance between them, making small tentative movements through the water toward Lars. Soon, they were close enough to touch, and even though he knew he'd get a snout full of salt water for his troubles, Lars did for Bangor what he'd done for Natalie just that morning. He gave the porpoise a big lick across the beak.

Hello, he was trying to say. *I love you. We're going to be okay.*

In response, Bangor rocked this way and that before emitting a warbling whistle—one that was music to Lars's ears. Gone were all the frightened frequencies of stress and confusion. In their place was a sweet tone of joy at seeing a good friend.

Okay, Lars thought. *That was the easy part. Now it gets harder.*

Hoping that his plan would work better than the humans' plan had, Lars looked Bangor in the eyes one more time—and then put his head down and swam straight into Bangor's side.

Thump! The porpoise's flank was soft and rubbery, but still heavy and solid, and Lars connected with it skull-first before bouncing backward through the water. Bangor, for his part, moved a few feet back in surprise, looking at Lars with an expression of confusion and concern. *You poor, non-swimming animal*, he seemed to be thinking. *Did you really mean to do that?*

But Lars had absolutely meant to, and now he intended to do it again. *Thump!* He swam right back into Bangor's side, and Bangor retreated a few more feet still. After one or two more repetitions, Bangor looked back in the direction Lars was pushing him—toward the *Maria P.*, where Mr. Prater watched, completely stunned—and then back at Lars. Then at the boat again. Then at Lars.

"Ruff!" Lars barked. *Now you're getting it.*

Tentatively, Bangor swam a few feet toward the boat. Lars wagged his tail hard enough to stir the water around him, and barked again.

The night they'd met, Bangor had saved Lars's life by leading him back into Perkins Cove. Now Lars would return the favor by leading Bangor out of it.

Natalie must have caught on at that point, because now Lars could feel her swimming past him, making her way back to the boat.

"Get ready to go, Dad!" she yelled up at her father. "And make sure everyone else is ready to go! But this time, they can only turn their boats on one at a time—and only on my signal!"

Meanwhile, Lars had paddled forward to catch up with Bangor, and together, the dog and porpoise were heading out to sea. By this point, Lars no longer had to physically push Bangor to get him to go where he wanted—in fact, Bangor helped nudge Lars around the side of the *Maria P.*—and then the two friends were out in open water. Here, Lars could no longer keep up with Bangor, and he didn't even try. The porpoise picked up speed and moved ten, twenty, and then thirty yards out.

"Bangor, wait!" Natalie cried from the boat, where she was dripping and wrapped in a towel. But as Lars slowed down and watched happily, his plan took hold. Bangor, realizing his friend was no longer right beside him, turned inquisitively to look back.

And he saw Lars and the *Maria P.*, and all the boats lined up beside and behind them.

And in that moment, even though they were a hundred feet apart, and Lars didn't speak porpoise, and Bangor didn't speak dog—despite all of that, Lars felt like they understood each other perfectly.

No longer worried that Bangor would swim off unaccompanied, Lars turned around and proudly paddled back to the side of the *Maria P.* The Praters gaped down at him, Natalie's expression one of love and pride, Mr. Prater's a mix of confusion and, nevertheless, admiration.

"Well," Mr. Prater said finally, "let's get that dog back onboard."

And as the girl Lars loved most in the world leaned down over the gunwale to help him scrabble back onboard, Mr. Prater headed back to the wheelhouse, yelling loudly enough for Lars, Natalie, and all the boats in the area to hear:

"We've got a porpoise to guide."

CHAPTER NINETEEN

Bangor

Bangor had to admit: Once Lars had coached him on it; and once Bangor had stopped questioning it; and once the boats of Perkins Cove had given him enough distance that their sounds weren't an assault on his ears . . . having someone else do your echolocation for you was a pretty sweet deal.

He didn't know how they were doing it—he'd never known that humans even *could* do it—but the farther they went up the shore, the clearer it became that the humans were working with some kind of echolocation that gave them a good idea of where Bangor needed to be going.

And at this point, they'd gone pretty darn far.

At first, Bangor hadn't totally understood. Since

Lars had pushed him out toward the sea, and slightly to the south, that was where Bangor had set out for. But shortly after that, he was met by a now-familiar sound: a pod of boats, pulling up and around him like a very wide net, far enough away that Bangor didn't feel threatened, but close enough that the message was clear: *No, not this way. Go another way.*

So he changed tack and chose a new direction, and as soon as he went too far in that direction, another pod of boats pulled up along his other side, as if to say, *Whoa, you overcorrected, try for something in the middle.*

Now Bangor understood why Natalie had enlisted so many boats. There was a whole lot of ocean out there for Bangor to get lost in, so it took a whole lot of people to keep him going in the direction they wanted.

Which, for the most part, seemed to be north. And then a little bit east. And then north again. And then west, hugging the shore, and then north, and then slightly east, and so on and so on, all the way up the coast, toward the place he had come from a couple of weeks ago, toward . . .

Home.

They were taking him home.

The moment he realized this, a thrill shot through Bangor's body, and he redoubled his swimming speed. This wasn't just some weird game, or some spur-of-the-moment day trip—this was an entire town working together to guide him safely back to the place where he'd come from. All around him, the endless drone of engines shifted into something that made sense, something he could understand and work with rather than flee from or fear. Soon Bangor was the solitary dot in the middle of a giant V of boats, urging him ever onward, northward, up the coast.

It was incredible. It felt like swimming with an entire tidal wave of power pushing him forward. It was as if there was a massive sea monster swimming right behind him, but the sea monster was cheering him on, and also had a gigantic motor engine strapped to its back.

And there was the *Maria P.*, working hard to stay alongside Bangor. And there were Lars and Natalie, watching whenever he breached to make sure he was still with them, whooping and cheering every time he came up for air.

As it turned out, their encouragement was very much needed. For the first hour or so, Bangor was sustained by the sheer excitement of the endeavor, and by the gratitude he felt for all these people who had come together to help him. By hour two or three of continuous swimming, though, monotony had started to set in, and just a bit of fatigue. Bangor had forgotten that the first trip down the coast had been tiring, an all-night marathon fueled largely by nerves and necessity.

Around hour four, Bangor noticed that certain boats were beginning to peel off from the group. Fishermen and lobstermen who, for one reason or another, had decided they'd had enough and returned to Ogunquit. Bangor didn't blame them, and he also didn't particularly mind. The fewer boats there were, the quieter it was, and the easier it was for him to echolocate normally. But he did feel a pang of envy for those humans who could just go home at the drop of a hat, relaxing on their boats as they did so. For him, going home was shaping up to be a grueling odyssey.

And come to think of it, he didn't even know if he was *really* going home.

Sure, the humans seemed to know where they were going. But how could they possibly know where his pod was? Bangor didn't even know himself. What if at the end of all this swimming, his worst fears came to pass, and he was left alone without either of his families?

No way. Natalie and Lars would never let that happen . . . right?

Hour five was full of these kinds of thoughts, and it was not a fun hour at all.

By hour six, Bangor wasn't sure he could go on anymore. He was swiftly becoming too tired, and the thought that he might be swimming to nowhere at all was too heavy on his mind. He tried to puff out a signal to Natalie or Lars, but Natalie just waved encouragingly. There were few enough boats now that Bangor could easily have heard Lars's barking over the engines, but even Lars was too tired to keep barking, and that, most of all, made Bangor feel exhausted. What could possibly lie ahead of him that was worth all this trouble?

Focusing his senses, Bangor released the strongest blast of echolocation he could muster up, straining to get as good a view of what was coming up as possible. If it was more of the same, he would just give up. He would stop here, and make a new home, or force the boats to turn around and slowly guide him back to Perkins Cove. All these thoughts flashed through his mind in a millisecond.

Just then, the clicks he'd sent out returned to him, mapping the sound of the ocean to come. The noise of the engine made everything a little blurry, but Bangor could still make out the basic shapes of what lay ahead.

There were some seagulls bobbing on the surface of the water.

There were some mackerel swimming a little way below them, trying to keep their distance from the seabirds.

And there, sneaking up on the mackerel, was a large and round figure, a slowly moving sphere of . . . a porpoise?

It couldn't be.

Bangor clicked again, this time pushing even

farther than the reach of his last survey, hardly daring to believe his initial senses. But sure enough, beyond the large and slow porpoise was another porpoise—a cute and tiny calf, eagerly chasing her companion.

And beyond that, a porpoise whose shape looked a lot like Bangor's, but slightly bigger, and slightly older.

And bringing up the rear, as always, a shape Bangor would know anywhere: the outline of a female porpoise, keeping a watchful eye over the members of her pod.

His pod.

It was Bangor's family.

Bangor wanted to jump for joy, and since he needed to breathe anyway, he did. Then he shot off a greeting. *"Eee-eee-ee-ee-e-e!"*

But the shapes in Bangor's vision didn't seem to notice. If anything, they seemed to be swimming farther away. No doubt they'd been spooked by the sounds of the engines that accompanied Bangor— the same sounds that now made it impossible for his family to hear him.

Or at least, for *one* of his families to hear him.

"Wroof!" There was Lars, appearing once more over the edge of the gunwale, sniffing furiously at the air and announcing his findings: *"Ruff, ruff!"*

"Dad!" Bangor heard Natalie yell. "Stop the boat! Something's happening—everyone, stop your boats!"

A swell of gratitude surged in Bangor's heart as, one by one, the engines around him fell silent and the boats fell behind, leaving him to chase after his pod. The only question was whether it would be soon enough. They were already getting farther away, and this time, a big whistle from Natalie might not be enough to bring any porpoises back.

Bangor had already swum a long distance that day, and the thought of swimming any farther, let alone any faster, made him ache all over. But as Lars's barking rang out behind him, he thought of everything his new pod had done to help him find his old pod. He didn't want any of their hard work to go to waste. And he wanted nothing more than for his two favorite families to meet—to tell Kittery all about his adventures with the fur turtle, and to introduce his little sister, Bristol, to his new friend Natalie.

So he did swim farther, and he did swim faster, and when his lungs were beginning to burn, he went up to the surface for one more big breath—*Puffff!*—then dove down and released the biggest welcome call of his life.

"*Eeee-eeee-eee-eee-ee-ee-e-e-e!*"

The sound shot over the dying sound waves of the boats and raced to nip at the flukes of his family.

And when his sounds returned to him, not milliseconds later, they brought an image he'd imagined for weeks: his mother, Kittery, turning in shock and amazement at seeing her son coming home at last.

"*Eee-eee-ee-ee-e-e!*" Bangor repeated, a little more weakly now that he was once more almost out of breath. As Kittery returned the call, everyone else in the pod turned around, too. They called out as well, and then they were all racing toward Bangor, and Bangor was able to fall still at last, letting waves of happy exhaustion wash over him as his pod surrounded him with their joyous sounds.

Any fears Bangor had that his family might have treated him differently after his long time away vanished the moment his older brother, Belfast, bashed brashly into his right flank, teasing him lovingly: *Where'd you go, bro? Did you get lost?*

"*Ree-ee-ee,*" scolded Kittery, nudging Belfast away and nuzzling her snout up against Bangor's. *We missed you. But where did you go?*

Bristol was too out-of-her-mind hyper to say much of anything coherent, zipping and circling around all of them like one of those darting fish Uncle York was always looking for. And speaking of Uncle York, there he was, swimming toward Bangor faster than Bangor had ever seen him swim. It wasn't very fast, but for Uncle York, it was practically zooming.

Their love reenergized Bangor, and by the time everyone had gotten their share of spinning and dipping and flipping and laughing, he was ready to share all the things he'd been hoping to share with them.

"*Sreee-ee-ee!*" he said. *You guys* have *to meet my new friends!*

Belfast laughed and chittered skeptically. *You made friends? I'll believe it when I see it.*

But Bristol had already shot past him, practically

sending Kittery into a panic as the youngest and friendliest member of the pod raced straight toward the boats that had brought Bangor home.

And there, leaning over the edge of the *Maria P.* to greet her, were Lars, barking happily, and Natalie, smiling the brightest smile Bangor had ever seen.

"*Ee-ee-ee?*" Kittery whistled, looking straight at Lars. *What is* that?

Bangor's snout split apart in a grin as he began the introductions.

<hr/>

It was the best day Bangor could ever remember, and porpoises tended to have some pretty good days. Belfast turned out to love showing off for the humans just as much as Bangor did—possibly even more. Natalie got in the water and made fast friends with Bristol, and by the end of the day, even Kittery was fond of the human girl. And once Uncle York realized what most of these boats were meant for—that was, for acquiring and storing fish—he stuck to them like a barnacle, with the same hopeful patience Bangor had seen Lars employ when humans brought food to the beach.

As for Lars, he was in and out of the water constantly, splashing and being splashed in turn by one porpoise after another, but by Bangor most of all. If Bangor was being honest, it was because he didn't want to say good-bye to Lars yet. To anyone, really, but to Lars most of all. None of this would have happened if Lars hadn't been in the water when Bangor first got to Perkins Cove. He'd been the best part of the worst day of Bangor's life, and now Lars was the most important part of the best day of Bangor's life. How did you say good-bye to someone like that? What did you do to show them how you cared?

Whatever it was, Bangor would have to figure it out soon. The sun was going down, and there weren't many onlookers left. Most of the other fishermen—as impressed as they'd been by Belfast's tricks and Uncle York's persistence—had gone home one by one, and now there were only a handful of boats remaining besides the *Maria P.* Even Lars and Natalie were clearly getting tired. Lars's paddling had slowed gradually as the sun got closer to the water, and Natalie was making sure they stuck nearer and nearer to the side of the *Maria P.*

"Bangor," Natalie said. Bangor recognized the human word for his name and turned toward her. "We have to go now."

Bangor couldn't understand the words, but he could absolutely understand the meaning behind them and the emotion that clogged Natalie's throat when she said them. Bangor felt those emotions, too, but as he watched Lars's paddling slow to a near halt, Bangor was reminded of the night they had met.

And just like that, he knew how to say good-bye.

"Ee-ee," he announced to his family. *Watch this.*

He swam cautiously up to Lars, nudging him gently away from the edge of the boat. Then, before Lars could react, Bangor dipped underwater, briefly, briskly, just long enough to position himself exactly where he wanted to be, and then . . .

He rose, and Lars rose with him, adjusting his stance until he had a good perch on Bangor's back, which didn't take that long. After all, this wasn't Lars's first ride.

Bangor had decided to say good-bye the exact same way he'd said hello.

Natalie laughed and clapped, and Mr. Prater roared, and the pod puffed with glee, and Mr. Reardon, Diver Bob, and all the other fishermen of Ogunquit stared in astonishment as Lars and Bangor took one more ride together.

And that was better than any good-bye.

CHAPTER TWENTY

Natalie

"I still think it's a bad idea."

"It's a great idea. He'll do great."

"He sees one tennis ball, or one croissant, and he'll be gone like a shot, and the whole thing will be ruined."

"Who brings a tennis ball to a wedding?"

"I wouldn't rule *you* out, for starters. Oh, no, he heard you say *tennis ball*."

Lars leaped up hopefully at Natalie, assuming a tennis ball was about to be thrown, and the pillow that had been carefully balanced on his back went flying.

"See," Mr. Prater said, trying but failing to hide his laughter. "If there had been a ring on that, it would be totally gone by now. Lost in the grass. Wedding ruined."

"We've still got some time," Natalie said, bending down to pick up the pillow and giving Lars a playful swat with it. "Besides, who else would you pick to be the ring bearer? Sammy Reardon? No way. He's even more distractible than Lars."

"You've got one day," Mr. Prater said. "I just don't want to be known as the man who ruined his ex-wife's wedding because he allowed a dog to—"

"Hello!" The woman in question had just poked her head through the door. "Sorry to eavesdrop, but the only way you will ruin my wedding is by being late to my rehearsal dinner. So if you wouldn't mind hurrying up, that would be—oh, Jim, you know you don't have to wear your suit for the rehearsal, right?"

"I wanted to show you I got it dry cleaned!" Mr. Prater proudly extended his arms, showing the lack of spots or wrinkles on the suit. "Business has been booming. No more Bran Crisps for me!"

"I don't know what that means," Natalie's mother

said. "But I'm happy for you. Now, come on, everyone, let's go."

The Praters—Natalie, her father, and Lars—followed Natalie's mom out of the back room of Barry Barnacle's Seafood and Restaurant.

"It's not the classiest place in the world," Natalie's mother had admitted at her bridal shower, "but it makes Bob happy, and that's what makes me happy."

It was clearly making Lars happy, too, as his head positively whipped around trying to catch all the seafood smells the caterers were carrying by.

"Mom," Natalie said, putting on her most persuasive voice. "You'd still like for Lars to be part of your wedding, right?"

"Oh, of course," her mother said, waving to Bob as they entered the dining room. "Lars is the reason we're all here. If you hadn't met him, and he hadn't met Bangor, and we hadn't all—well, you know—who knows if we'd all be standing here, happy, together, right now?"

"Well, I'm *sitting* here," Bob said as they approached. "And I'm ready to eat!" Natalie groaned, but she didn't roll her eyes—she'd gotten a lot better about not rolling her eyes—and the future Maria Dugnutt laughed a full, genuine belly laugh.

"I can't believe you're going to be in the wedding," Mr. Prater muttered to Lars as they all sat down for dinner.

"You asked for it when you adopted him," Nancy Jane said, a few seats down. "Isn't that right, Mark?"

"As a public official, I can offer no comment," said Mayor Maher, sitting next to Nancy Jane and blushing furiously, as he always did at her remarks. When Nancy Jane and Mayor Maher first started seeing each other, the mayor's constant blushing had made Natalie worried for their future as a couple. But now that it had been four months, she was pretty sure it was just what he did when he was around her, or talking about her, or looking at one of the many paintings that he'd bought from her or commissioned from her or taken from her studio and hung all over town hall.

It had been an odd summer.

It had also been the best summer of Natalie's life.

Adopting Lars had just been the start of it. Saying

good-bye to Bangor was bittersweet, but their fare-well had unexpected—and dramatic—consequences. It turned out that a crewmember on Mr. Grundy's boat had recorded a video of Lars and Bangor's last ride together on his phone, and once it went public, things got crazy fast. It was hard to remember now what order things had happened in. Had it gone local news, Internet, then national news? Or had it started on the Internet, and then the local news, and then the national news? Either way, soon everyone was talking about the dog riding the porpoise in the middle of the Atlantic Ocean, and the humans who were responsi-ble for both.

The *Maria P.* could clearly be made out in the video, name and all, and soon Mr. Prater's business really was booming. Everyone wanted to buy their fish from Ogunquit's most famous fisherman. And when a nightly news piece played up Mr. Prater as a single father just doing his best to keep up with his daughter's love of animals, different kinds of offers came pouring in from lots of single women, with lots of interest in Natalie's father. But he was a little too busy with business to focus on dating right now, especially once Barry Rosenberg asked him to be the main vendor for Barnacle Barry's Seafood and Restaurant. In just one summer, everyone in town had stopped thinking of Natalie's dad as the poor single dad; now they thought of him as the successful, sought-after businessman who was providing the fish for his ex-wife's wedding, which was a little weird, but still pretty nice.

And Natalie's life hadn't been too rough, either. She'd made quite a bit of money that summer babysitting Sam Reardon, who'd been ruined for other babysitters forever by the fact that none of them had an amazing dog. Furthermore, fame had come with its own set of benefits for her. She'd never exactly been unpopular at school, but being the girl in the news with the porpoise-riding dog still opened up all sorts of new social windows. When a few girls from the swim team had asked her for her autograph, she'd struck up a conversation with them, and they'd quickly become friends. Now she was swimming with them regularly, and planning to try out for the swim team in a few weeks.

Between babysitting, swimming, and going out on her father's boat, Natalie barely had any free time during the week. But what time she did have, she used it for weekly dinners with her mother. After all the time they'd spent apart, they were now closer than ever; the distance followed by reconciliation had allowed them to talk about all sorts of things they'd never talked about before. Once tourist season got into full swing, she even accompanied her mother a few times as guests of honor on Diver Bob's Sea Life Tours. It was on one of these tours that Diver—that *Bob*—had gotten down on one knee, snorkel still on his face, and asked Natalie's mother to marry him. And it was on that same tour that Natalie's mother had instantly turned and asked Natalie to be her bridesmaid. Natalie, to her excitement and slight amazement, had said yes.

And now here they all were, just past the dying days of tourist season, preparing for what looked to be a beautiful October wedding. Lars sat under the table, gnawing on a chunk of lobster. Nancy Jane took some lobster for herself and fed some of it to Mayor Maher, whispering something in his ear that made him blush harder than ever. Mr. Prater chatted happily with Barry Rosenberg about final details for tomorrow. And Natalie's mother laughed uproariously at something her fiancé had said, her mouth full of lobster. Even though it was gross in a couple of ways, mostly it just made Natalie smile. Her mother had gone where the joy of life had taken her.

Everything was perfect.

Or almost perfect.

Every time Natalie saw a reminder of Bangor, she still felt a stab of loss, and a curiosity about what her friend might be doing now. And after the success of Nancy Jane's art show, reminders of Bangor hung everywhere around town. Natalie was glad she had Lars, and her father, and the rest of her family, but she couldn't help but feel like one member of her family was missing.

Her thoughts, and not to mention the entire rehearsal dinner, were interrupted by an unexpected and violent knocking on the front door of Barnacle Barry's—a knocking that oddly seemed to be coming from very close to the ground.

"What in the world . . . ?" Natalie's mother said, but Natalie was already headed to the door, with Lars following curiously behind her.

"Sam Reardon," Natalie said wearily, pulling open the door to reveal the frantic child. "What could *possibly* be so important that—"

"He's back he's back he's back he's back he's back!!!" Sam yelled, jumping up and down in great, manic hops.

Natalie's jaw dropped. She heard a clatter of silverware behind her. She turned and saw that every single adult at the dining table had stood up, staring at her and Sam.

"You don't think . . ." she began.

"Go!" Nancy Jane urged. *"Go!"*

Natalie turned back around and saw that Sam was already running toward the beach. That was all she needed to know.

"Come on, Lars!" she said, and she followed Sam right out the door.

"I just bought you that dress!" Mr. Prater yelled after her. *"Don't get it wet*—oh, what's the use. Come on, we'd better follow her."

The dress in question flapped around Natalie's knees as she ran to the beach, as fast as her legs could carry her. It was the fastest she'd ever run since that Sunday morning in April when Lars had led her down Main Street, just as Sam was leading them now—over the cobblestones, past the Coveside Café, past the town hall—all the way to Perkins Cove, where a crowd of the year's last tourists, and a few Ogunquit townspeople, were already waiting for her.

"There you are!" said Mrs. Reardon when she saw Sam and Natalie scrambling down the rocks. "I told him to go as fast as he could—by the way, are you free to babysit on Thursday, or—"

"Mrs. Reardon," Natalie interrupted her breathlessly. "What's going *on*?!" She was almost certain she knew the answer, but she wanted to hear it for herself. And before Mrs. Reardon could say anything, Natalie heard exactly the answer she was looking for:

Puff!

Natalie whirled. Sam jumped up and down and yelled incomprehensibly. Lars did the same, but in dog language.

And there, in the chilly October waters of Perkins Cove, was Bangor, smiling cheekily at Natalie, just waiting for someone to come in and play with him.

Wait, no. There was already someone—or some*things*—in there with him.

Puff! Puff!

"It's his family," Natalie said as Mr. Prater and the other members of the wedding party finally arrived on the beach behind her, panting and out of breath. "He brought his whole pod!"

There was a little porpoise, zooming around curiously; two larger porpoises, hanging back but clearly intrigued by the mass of humanity on the beach; and the largest, laziest porpoise Natalie had ever seen.

But before she could process any of that, or decide what to do next, Lars decided for everyone. He ran straight down the beach, raced over the surf, and splashed hard and fast into the water.

And as she followed Lars into the water, completely

soaking her new dress, Natalie felt like, at long last, every member of her family was together. It was a big family, and an odd one, and sometimes she didn't see people in it for a while, and sometimes the people in her family weren't even people. But they were all hers, and she loved them. They were her good thing.

And she jumped in.

About the Author

M. C. Ross is an author and playwright living in New York City. He has one dog and too many fish, and he loves writing about animals almost as much as he loves spending time with them. This is his second book for young readers.